The ABC Murders

Agatha Christie is kn [illegible] of Crime. Her books [illegible] with another billion [illegible] widely published au [illegible] only by the Bible and Sha [illegible] 0 crime novels and short story collec [illegible] ix novels written under the name of Mary Westma [illegible]

Agatha Christie's first novel, *The Mysterious Affair at Styles*, was written towards the end of the First World War, in which she served as a VAD. In it she created Hercule Poirot, the little Belgian detective who was destined to become the most popular detective in crime fiction since Sherlock Holmes. It was eventually published by The Bodley Head in 1920.

In 1926, after averaging a book a year, Agatha Christie wrote her masterpiece. *The Murder of Roger Ackroyd* was the first of her books to be published by Collins and marked the beginning of an author-publisher relationship which lasted for 50 years and well over 70 books. *The Murder of Roger Ackroyd* was also the first of Agatha Christie's books to be dramatised – under the name *Alibi* – and to have a successful run in London's West End. *The Mousetrap*, her most famous play of all, opened in 1952 and is the longest-running play in history.

Agatha Christie was made a Dame in 1971. She died in 1976, since when a number of books have been published posthumously: the bestselling novel *Sleeping Murder* appeared later that year, followed by her autobiography and the short story collections *Miss Marple's Final Cases*, *Problem at Pollensa Bay* and *While the Light Lasts*. In 1998 *Black Coffee* was the first of her plays to be novelised by another author, Charles Osborne.

The Agatha Christie Collection

The Man In The Brown Suit
The Secret of Chimneys
The Seven Dials Mystery
The Mysterious Mr Quin
The Sittaford Mystery
The Hound of Death
The Listerdale Mystery
Why Didn't They Ask Evans?
Parker Pyne Investigates
Murder Is Easy
And Then There Were None
Towards Zero
Death Comes as the End
Sparkling Cyanide
Crooked House
They Came to Baghdad
Destination Unknown
Spider's Web *
The Unexpected Guest *
Ordeal by Innocence
The Pale Horse
Endless Night
Passenger To Frankfurt
Problem at Pollensa Bay
While the Light Lasts

Poirot

The Mysterious Affair at Styles
The Murder on the Links
Poirot Investigates
The Murder of Roger Ackroyd
The Big Four
The Mystery of the Blue Train
Black Coffee *
Peril at End House
Lord Edgware Dies
Murder on the Orient Express
Three-Act Tragedy
Death in the Clouds
The ABC Murders
Murder in Mesopotamia
Cards on the Table
Murder in the Mews
Dumb Witness
Death on the Nile
Appointment With Death
Hercule Poirot's Christmas
Sad Cypress
One, Two, Buckle My Shoe
Evil Under the Sun
Five Little Pigs
The Hollow
The Labours of Hercules
Taken at the Flood
Mrs McGinty's Dead
After the Funeral
Hickory Dickory Dock
Dead Man's Folly
Cat Among the Pigeons
The Adventure of the Christmas Pudding
The Clocks
Third Girl
Hallowe'en Party
Elephants Can Remember
Poirot's Early Cases
Curtain: Poirot's Last Case

Marple

The Murder at the Vicarage
The Thirteen Problems
The Body in the Library
The Moving Finger
A Murder is Announced
They Do It With Mirrors
A Pocket Full of Rye
The 4.50 from Paddington
The Mirror Crack'd from Side to Side
A Caribbean Mystery
At Bertram's Hotel
Nemesis
Sleeping Murder
Miss Marple's Final Cases

Tommy & Tuppence

The Secret Adversary
Partners in Crime
N or M?
By the Pricking of My Thumbs
Postern of Fate

Published as Mary Westmacott

Giant's Bread
Unfinished Portrait
Absent in the Spring
The Rose and the Yew Tree
A Daughter's a Daughter
The Burden

Memoirs

An Autobiography
Come, Tell Me How You Live

Play Collections

The Mousetrap and Selected Plays
Witness for the Prosecution and Selected Plays

* novelised by Charles Osborne

Agatha Christie

The ABC Murders

HARPER

This edition produced for The Book People Ltd,
Hall Wood Avenue, Haydock, St Helens, WA11 9UL

HARPER

An imprint of HarperCollins*Publishers*
77–85 Fulham Palace Road
Hammersmith, London W6 8JB
www.harpercollins.co.uk

This *Agatha Christie Signature Edition* published 2007
1

First published in Great Britain by
Collins 1936

ISBN 978 0 00 781557 9

Typeset by Palimpsest Book Production Limited,
Grangemouth, Stirlingshire

Printed and bound in Great Britain by
Clays Ltd, St Ives plc

To James Watts

One of my most sympathetic readers

Contents

Foreword

By Captain Arthur Hastings, O.B.E.

In this narrative of mine I have departed from my usual practice of relating only those incidents and scenes at which I myself was present. Certain chapters, therefore, are written in the third person.

I wish to assure my readers that I can vouch for the occurrences related in these chapters. If I have taken a certain poetic licence in describing the thoughts and feelings of various persons, it is because I believe I have set them down with a reasonable amount of accuracy. I may add that they have been 'vetted' by my friend Hercule Poirot himself.

In conclusion, I will say that if I have described at too great length some of the secondary personal relationships which arose as a consequence of this strange series of crimes, it is because the human and personal elements can never be ignored. Hercule Poirot once taught me in a very dramatic manner that romance can be a by-product of crime.

As to the solving of the ABC mystery, I can only say that in my opinion Poirot showed real genius in the way he tackled a problem entirely unlike any which had previously come his way.

Chapter 1

The Letter

It was in June of 1935 that I came home from my ranch in South America for a stay of about six months. It had been a difficult time for us out there. Like everyone else, we had suffered from world depression. I had various affairs to see to in England that I felt could only be successful if a personal touch was introduced. My wife remained to manage the ranch.

I need hardly say that one of my first actions on reaching England was to look up my old friend, Hercule Poirot.

I found him installed in one of the newest type of service flats in London. I accused him (and he admitted the fact) of having chosen this particular building entirely on account of its strictly geometrical appearance and proportions.

'But yes, my friend, it is of a most pleasing symmetry, do you not find it so?'

I said that I thought there could be too much squareness and, alluding to an old joke, I asked if in this super-modern hostelry they managed to induce hens to lay square eggs.

Poirot laughed heartily.

'Ah, you remember that? Alas! no – science has not yet induced the hens to conform to modern tastes, they still lay eggs of different sizes and colours!'

I examined my old friend with an affectionate eye. He was looking wonderfully well – hardly a day older than when I had last seen him.

'You're looking in fine fettle, Poirot,' I said. 'You've hardly aged at all. In fact, if it were possible, I should say that you had fewer grey hairs than when I saw you last.'

Poirot beamed on me.

'And why is that not possible? It is quite true.'

'Do you mean your hair is turning from grey to black instead of from black to grey?'

'Precisely.'

'But surely that's a scientific impossibility!'

'Not at all.'

'But that's very extraordinary. It seems against nature.'

'As usual, Hastings, you have the beautiful and unsuspicious mind. Years do not change that in you! You perceive a fact and mention the solution of it in the same breath without noticing that you are doing so!'

I stared at him, puzzled.

Without a word he walked into his bedroom and returned with a bottle in his hand which he handed to me.

I took it, for the moment uncomprehending.

It bore the words:

Revivit. – To bring back the natural tone of the hair. *Revivit* is *not* a dye. In five shades, Ash, Chestnut, Titian, Brown, Black.

'Poirot,' I cried. 'You have dyed your hair!'

'Ah, the comprehension comes to you!'

'So *that's* why your hair looks so much blacker than it did last time I was back.'

'Exactly.'

'Dear me,' I said, recovering from the shock. 'I suppose next time I come home I shall find you wearing false moustaches – or are you doing so now?'

Poirot winced. His moustaches had always been his sensitive point. He was inordinately proud of them. My words touched him on the raw.

'No, no, indeed, *mon ami.* That day, I pray the good God, is still far off. The false moustache! *Quel horreur!*'

He tugged at them vigorously to assure me of their genuine character.

'Well, they are very luxuriant still,' I said.

'*N'est ce pas?* Never, in the whole of London, have I seen a pair of moustaches to equal mine.'

A good job too, I thought privately. But I would not for the world have hurt Poirot's feelings by saying so.

Instead I asked if he still practised his profession on occasion.

'I know,' I said, 'that you actually retired years ago –'

'*C'est vrai.* To grow the vegetable marrows! And immediately a murder occurs – and I send the vegetable marrows to promenade themselves to the devil. And since then – I know very well what you will say – I am like the prima donna who makes positively the farewell performance! That farewell performance, it repeats itself an indefinite number of times!'

I laughed.

'In truth, it has been very like that. Each time I say: this is the end. But no, something else arises! And I will admit it, my friend, the retirement I care for it not at all. If the little grey cells are not exercised, they grow the rust.'

'I see,' I said. 'You exercise them in moderation.'

'Precisely. I pick and choose. For Hercule Poirot nowadays only the cream of crime.'

'Has there been much cream about?'

'*Pas mal.* Not long ago I had a narrow escape.'

'Of failure?'

'No, no.' Poirot looked shocked. 'But I – *I, Hercule Poirot,* was nearly exterminated.'

I whistled.

'An enterprising murderer!'

'Not so much enterprising as careless,' said Poirot. 'Precisely that – careless. But let us not talk of it. You know, Hastings, in many ways I regard you as my mascot.'

'Indeed?' I said. 'In what ways?'

Poirot did not answer my question directly. He went on:

'As soon as I heard you were coming over I said to myself: something will arise. As in former days we will hunt together, we two. But if so it must be no common affair. It must be something' – he waved his hands excitedly – 'something *recherché* – delicate – *fine* . . .' He gave the last untranslatable word its full flavour.

'Upon my word, Poirot,' I said. 'Anyone would think you were ordering a dinner at the Ritz.'

'Whereas one cannot command a crime to order? Very true.' He sighed. 'But I believe in luck – in destiny, if you will. It is your destiny to stand beside me and prevent me from committing the unforgivable error.'

'What do you call the unforgivable error?'

'Overlooking the obvious.'

I turned this over in my mind without quite seeing the point.

'Well,' I said presently, smiling, 'has this super crime turned up yet?'

'*Pas encore.* At least – that is –'

He paused. A frown of perplexity creased his forehead. His hands automatically straightened an object or two that I had inadvertently pushed awry.

'I am not sure,' he said slowly.

There was something so odd about his tone that I looked at him in surprise.

The frown still lingered.

Suddenly with a brief decisive nod of the head he crossed the room to a desk near the window. Its contents, I need hardly say, were all neatly docketed and pigeon-holed so that he was able at once to lay his hand upon the paper he wanted.

He came slowly across to me, an open letter in his hand. He read it through himself, then passed it to me.

'Tell me, *mon ami*,' he said. 'What do you make of this?'

I took it from him with some interest.

It was written on thickish white notepaper in printed characters:

> *Mr Hercule Poirot, – You fancy yourself, don't you, at solving mysteries that are too difficult for our poor thick-headed British police? Let us see, Mr Clever Poirot,*

just how clever you can be. Perhaps you'll find this nut too hard to crack. Look out for Andover, on the 21st of the month.

Yours, etc.,
A B C.

I glanced at the envelope. That also was printed.

'Postmarked WC1,' said Poirot as I turned my attention to the postmark. 'Well, what is your opinion?'

I shrugged my shoulders as I handed it back to him.

'Some madman or other, I suppose.'

'That is all you have to say?'

'Well – doesn't it sound like a madman to you?'

'Yes, my friend, it does.'

His tone was grave. I looked at him curiously.

'You take this very seriously, Poirot.'

'A madman, *mon ami*, is to be taken seriously. A madman is a very dangerous thing.'

'Yes, of course, that is true . . . I hadn't considered that point . . . But what I meant was, it sounds more like a rather idiotic kind of hoax. Perhaps some convivial idiot who had had one over the eight.'

'*Comment?* Nine? Nine what?'

'Nothing – just an expression. I meant a fellow who was tight. No, damn it, a fellow who had had a spot too much to drink.'

'*Merci*, Hastings – the expression "tight" I *am* acquainted with it. As you say, there may be nothing more to it than that . . .'

'But you think there is?' I asked, struck by the dissatisfaction of his tone.

Poirot shook his head doubtfully, but he did not speak.

'What have you done about it?' I inquired.

'What can one do? I showed it to Japp. He was of the same opinion as you – a stupid hoax – that was the expression he used. They get these things every day at Scotland Yard. I, too, have had my share . . .'

'But you take this one seriously?'

Poirot replied slowly.

'There is something about that letter, Hastings, that I do not like . . .'

In spite of myself, his tone impressed me.

'You think – what?'

He shook his head, and picking up the letter, put it away again in the desk.

'If you really take it seriously, can't you do something?' I asked.

'As always, the man of action! But what is there to do? The county police have seen the letter but they, too, do not take it seriously. There are no fingerprints on it. There are no local clues as to the possible writer.'

'In fact there is only your own instinct?'

'Not instinct, Hastings. Instinct is a bad word. It is my *knowledge* – my *experience* – that tells me that something about that letter is wrong –'

He gesticulated as words failed him, then shook his head again.

'I may be making the mountain out of the anthill. In any case there is nothing to be done but wait.'

'Well, the 21st is Friday. If a whacking great robbery takes place near Andover then –'

'Ah, what a comfort that would be –!'

'*A comfort*?' I stared. The word seemed to be a very extraordinary one to use.

'A robbery may be a *thrill* but it can hardly be a comfort!' I protested.

Poirot shook his head energetically.

'You are in error, my friend. You do not understand my meaning. A robbery would be a relief since it would dispossess my mind of the fear of something else.'

'Of what?'

'*Murder*,' said Hercule Poirot.

Chapter 2

Not from Captain Hastings' Personal Narrative

Mr Alexander Bonaparte Cust rose from his seat and peered near-sightedly round the shabby bedroom. His back was stiff from sitting in a cramped position and as he stretched himself to his full height an onlooker would have realized that he was, in reality, quite a tall man. His stoop and his near-sighted peering gave a delusive impression.

Going to a well-worn overcoat hanging on the back of the door, he took from the pocket a packet of cheap cigarettes and some matches. He lit a cigarette and then returned to the table at which he had been sitting. He picked up a railway guide and consulted it, then he returned to the consideration of a typewritten list of names. With a pen, he made a tick against one of the first names on the list.

It was Thursday, June 20th.

Chapter 3

Andover

I had been impressed at the time by Poirot's forebodings about the anonymous letter he had received, but I must admit that the matter had passed from my mind when the 21st actually arrived and the first reminder of it came with a visit paid to my friend by Chief Inspector Japp of Scotland Yard. The CID inspector had been known to us for many years and he gave me a hearty welcome.

'Well, I never,' he exclaimed. 'If it isn't Captain Hastings back from the wilds of the what do you call it! Quite like old days seeing you here with Monsieur Poirot. You're looking well, too. Just a little bit thin on top, eh? Well, that's what we're all coming to. I'm the same.'

I winced slightly. I was under the impression that owing to the careful way I brushed my hair across the top of my head the thinness referred to by Japp was quite unnoticeable. However, Japp had never been remarkable for tact where I was concerned, so I put a good face upon it and agreed that we were none of us getting any younger.

'Except Monsieur Poirot here,' said Japp. 'Quite a good advertisement for a hair tonic, he'd be. Face fungus sprouting finer than ever. Coming out into the limelight, too, in his old age. Mixed up in all the celebrated cases of the day. Train mysteries, air mysteries, high society deaths – oh, he's here, there and everywhere. Never been so celebrated as since he retired.'

'I have already told Hastings that I am like the prima donna who makes always one more appearance,' said Poirot, smiling.

'I shouldn't wonder if you ended by detecting your own death,' said Japp, laughing heartily. 'That's an idea, that is. Ought to be put in a book.'

'It will be Hastings who will have to do that,' said Poirot, twinkling at me.

'Ha ha! That would be a joke, that would,' laughed Japp.

I failed to see why the idea was so extremely amusing, and in any case I thought the joke was in poor taste. Poirot, poor old chap, is getting on. Jokes about his approaching demise can hardly be agreeable to him.

Perhaps my manner showed my feelings, for Japp changed the subject.

'Have you heard about Monsieur Poirot's anonymous letter?'

'I showed it to Hastings the other day,' said my friend.

'Of course,' I exclaimed. 'It had quite slipped my memory. Let me see, what was the date mentioned?'

'The 21st,' said Japp. 'That's what I dropped in about. Yesterday was the 21st and just out of curiosity I rang up Andover last night. It was a hoax all right. Nothing doing. One broken shop window – kid throwing stones – and a couple of drunk and disorderlies. So just for once our Belgian friend was barking up the wrong tree.'

'I am relieved, I must confess,' acknowledged Poirot.

'You'd quite got the wind up about it, hadn't you?' said Japp affectionately. 'Bless you, we get dozens of letters like that coming in every day! People with nothing better to do and a bit weak in the top storey sit down and write 'em. They don't mean any harm! Just a kind of excitement.'

'I have indeed been foolish to take the matter so seriously,' said Poirot. 'It is the nest of the horse that I put my nose into there.'

'You're mixing up mares and wasps,' said Japp.

'*Pardon?*'

'Just a couple of proverbs. Well, I must be off. Got a little business in the next street to see to – receiving stolen jewellery. I thought I'd just drop in on my way and put your mind at rest. Pity to let those grey cells function unnecessarily.'

With which words and a hearty laugh, Japp departed.

'He does not change much, the good Japp, eh?' asked Poirot.

'He looks much older,' I said. 'Getting as grey as a badger,' I added vindictively.

Poirot coughed and said:

'You know, Hastings, there is a little device – my hairdresser is a man of great ingenuity – one attaches it to the scalp and brushes one's own hair over it – it is not a wig, you comprehend – but –'

'Poirot,' I roared. 'Once and for all I will have nothing to do with the beastly inventions of your confounded hairdresser. What's the matter with the top of my head?'

'Nothing – nothing at all.'

'It's not as though I were going *bald*.'

'Of course not! Of course not!'

'The hot summers out there naturally cause the hair to fall out a bit. I shall take back a really good hair tonic.'

'*Précisément*.'

'And, anyway, what business is it of Japp's? He

always was an offensive kind of devil. And no sense of humour. The kind of man who laughs when a chair is pulled away just as a man is about to sit down.'

'A great many people would laugh at that.'

'It's utterly senseless.'

'From the point of view of the man about to sit, certainly it is.'

'Well,' I said, slightly recovering my temper. (I admit that I am touchy about the thinness of my hair.) 'I'm sorry that anonymous letter business came to nothing.'

'I have indeed been in the wrong over that. About that letter, therc was, I thought, the odour of the fish. Instead a mere stupidity. Alas, I grow old and suspicious like the blind watch-dog who growls when there is nothing there.'

'If I'm going to co-operate with you, we must look about for some other "creamy" crime,' I said with a laugh.

'You remember your remark of the other day? If you could order a crime as one orders a dinner, what would you choose?'

I fell in with his humour.

'Let me see now. Let's review the menu. Robbery? Forgery? No, I think not. Rather too vegetarian. It must be murder – red-blooded murder – with trimmings, of course.'

'Naturally. The *hors d'oeuvres*.'

'Who shall the victim be – man or woman? Man, I think. Some big-wig. American millionaire. Prime Minister. Newspaper proprietor. Scene of the crime – well, what's wrong with the good old library? Nothing like it for atmosphere. As for the weapon – well, it might be a curiously twisted dagger – or some blunt instrument – a carved stone idol –'

Poirot sighed.

'Or, of course,' I said, 'there's poison – but that's always so technical. Or a revolver shot echoing in the night. Then there must be a beautiful girl or two –'

'With auburn hair,' murmured my friend.

'Your same old joke. One of the beautiful girls, of course, must be unjustly suspected – and there's some misunderstanding between her and the young man. And then, of course, there must be some other suspects – an older woman – dark, dangerous type – and some friend or rival of the dead man's – and a quiet secretary – dark horse – and a hearty man with a bluff manner – and a couple of discharged servants or gamekeepers or somethings – and a damn fool of a detective rather like Japp – and well – that's about all.'

'That is your idea of the cream, eh?'

'I gather you don't agree.'

Poirot looked at me sadly.

'You have made there a very pretty résumé of nearly all the detective stories that have ever been written.'

'Well,' I said. 'What would *you* order?'

Poirot closed his eyes and leaned back in his chair. His voice came purringly from between his lips.

'A very simple crime. A crime with no complications. A crime of quiet domestic life . . . very unimpassioned – very *intime*.'

'How can a crime be *intime*?'

'Supposing,' murmured Poirot, 'that four people sit down to play bridge and one, the odd man out, sits in a chair by the fire. At the end of the evening the man by the fire is found dead. One of the four, while he is dummy, has gone over and killed him, and intent on the play of the hand, the other three have not noticed. Ah, there would be a crime for you! *Which of the four was it?*'

'Well,' I said. 'I can't see *any* excitement in that!'

Poirot threw me a glance of reproof.

'No, because there are no curiously twisted daggers, no blackmail, no emerald that is the stolen eye of a god, no untraceable Eastern poisons. You have the melodramatic soul, Hastings. You would like, not one murder, but a series of murders.'

'I admit,' I said, 'that a second murder in a book often cheers things up. If the murder happens in the first chapter, and you have to follow up everybody's alibi until the last page but one – well, it does get a bit tedious.'

The telephone rang and Poirot rose to answer.

''Allo,' he said. ''Allo. Yes, it is Hercule Poirot speaking.'

He listened for a minute or two and then I saw his face change.

His own side of the conversation was short and disjointed.

'*Mais oui* . . .'

'Yes, of course . . .'

'But yes, we will come . . .'

'Naturally . . .'

'It may be as you say . . .'

'Yes, I will bring it. *A tout à l'heure* then.'

He replaced the receiver and came across the room to me.

'That was Japp speaking, Hastings.'

'Yes?'

'He had just got back to the Yard. There was a message from Andover . . .'

'Andover?' I cried excitedly.

Poirot said slowly:

'An old woman of the name of Ascher who keeps a little tobacco and newspaper shop has been found murdered.'

I think I felt ever so slightly damped. My interest, quickened by the sound of Andover, suffered a faint check. I had expected something fantastic – out of the way! The murder of an old woman who kept a little tobacco shop seemed, somehow, sordid and uninteresting.

Poirot continued in the same slow, grave voice:

'The Andover police believe they can put their hand on the man who did it –'

I felt a second throb of disappointment.

'It seems the woman was on bad terms with her husband. He drinks and is by way of being rather a nasty customer. He's threatened to take her life more than once.

'Nevertheless,' continued Poirot, 'in view of what has happened, the police there would like to have another look at the anonymous letter I received. I have said that you and I will go down to Andover at once.'

My spirits revived a little. After all, sordid as this crime seemed to be, it was a *crime*, and it was a long time since I had had any association with crime and criminals.

I hardly listened to the next words Poirot said. But they were to come back to me with significance later.

'This is the beginning,' said Hercule Poirot.

Chapter 4

Mrs Ascher

We were received at Andover by Inspector Glen, a tall fair-haired man with a pleasant smile.

For the sake of conciseness I think I had better give a brief résumé of the bare facts of the case.

The crime was discovered by Police Constable Dover at 1 am on the morning of the 22nd. When on his round he tried the door of the shop and found it unfastened, he entered and at first thought the place was empty. Directing his torch over the counter, however, he caught sight of the huddled-up body of the old woman. When the police surgeon arrived on the spot it was elicited that the woman had been struck down by a heavy blow on the back of the head, probably while she was reaching down a packet of cigarettes from the shelf behind the counter. Death must have occurred about nine to seven hours previously.

'But we've been able to get it down a bit nearer than

that,' explained the inspector. 'We've found a man who went in and bought some tobacco at 5.30. And a second man went in and found the shop empty, as he thought, at five minutes past six. That puts the time at between 5.30 and 6.5. So far I haven't been able to find anyone who saw this man Ascher in the neighbourhood, but, of course, it's early as yet. He was in the Three Crowns at nine o'clock pretty far gone in drink. When we get hold of him he'll be detained on suspicion.'

'Not a very desirable character, inspector?' asked Poirot.

'Unpleasant bit of goods.'

'He didn't live with his wife?'

'No, they separated some years ago. Ascher's a German. He was a waiter at one time, but he took to drink and gradually became unemployable. His wife went into service for a bit. Her last place was as cook-housekeeper to an old lady, Miss Rose. She allowed her husband so much out of her wages to keep himself, but he was always getting drunk and coming round and making scenes at the places where she was employed. That's why she took the post with Miss Rose at The Grange. It's three miles out of Andover, dead in the country. He couldn't get at her there so well. When Miss Rose died, she left Mrs Ascher a small legacy, and the woman started this tobacco and newsagent business – quite a tiny place – just cheap cigarettes and a few newspapers – that sort of thing. She just about managed to keep going. Ascher used to come round and abuse her now and again and she used to give him a bit to get rid of him. She allowed him fifteen shillings a week regular.'

'Had they any children?' asked Poirot.

'No. There's a niece. She's in service near Overton. Very superior, steady young woman.'

'And you say this man Ascher used to threaten his wife?'

'That's right. He was a terror when he was in drink – cursing and swearing that he'd bash her head in. She had a hard time, did Mrs Ascher.'

'What age of woman was she?'

'Close on sixty – respectable and hard-working.'

Poirot said gravely:

'It is your opinion, inspector, that this man Ascher committed the crime?'

The inspector coughed cautiously.

'It's a bit early to say that, Mr Poirot, but I'd like to hear Franz Ascher's own account of how he spent yesterday evening. If he can give a satisfactory account of himself, well and good – if not –'

His pause was a pregnant one.

'Nothing was missing from the shop?'

'Nothing. Money in the till quite undisturbed. No signs of robbery.'

'You think that this man Ascher came into the shop drunk, started abusing his wife and finally struck her down?'

'It seems the most likely solution. But I must confess, sir, I'd like to have another look at that very odd letter you received. I was wondering if it was just possible that it came from this man Ascher.'

Poirot handed over the letter and the inspector read it with a frown.

'It doesn't read like Ascher,' he said at last. 'I doubt if Ascher would use the term "our" British police – not unless he was trying to be extra cunning – and I doubt if he's got the wits for that. Then the man's a wreck – all to pieces. His hand's too shaky to print letters clearly like this. It's good quality notepaper and ink, too. It's odd that the letter should mention the 21st of the month. Of course it *might* be coincidence.'

'That is possible – yes.'

'But I don't like this kind of coincidence, Mr Poirot. It's a bit too pat.'

He was silent for a minute or two – a frown creasing his forehead.

'A B C. Who the devil could A B C be? We'll see if Mary Drower (that's the niece) can give us any help. It's an odd business. But for this letter I'd have put my money on Franz Ascher for a certainty.'

'Do you know anything of Mrs Ascher's past?'

'She's a Hampshire woman. Went into service as a girl up in London – that's where she met Ascher and married him. Things must have been difficult for them during the war. She actually left him for good in 1922. They were in London then. She came back here to get away from him, but he got wind of where she was and followed her down here, pestering her for money–' A constable came in. 'Yes, Briggs, what is it?'

'It's the man Ascher, sir. We've brought him in.'

'Right. Bring him in here. Where was he?'

'Hiding in a truck on the railway siding.'

'He was, was he? Bring him along.'

Franz Ascher was indeed a miserable and unprepossessing specimen. He was blubbering and cringing and blustering alternately. His bleary eyes moved shiftily from one face to another.

'What do you want with me? I have not done nothing. It is a shame and a scandal to bring me here! You are swine, how dare you?' His manner changed suddenly. 'No, no, I do not mean that – you would not hurt a poor old man – not be hard on him. Everyone is hard on poor old Franz. Poor old Franz.'

Mr Ascher started to weep.

'That'll do, Ascher,' said the inspector. 'Pull yourself together. I'm not charging you with anything – yet. And you're not bound to make a statement unless you like. On the other hand, if you're *not* concerned in the murder of your wife –'

Ascher interrupted him – his voice rising to a scream.

'I did not kill her! I did not kill her! It is all lies! You are goddamned English pigs – all against me. I never kill her – never.'

'You threatened to often enough, Ascher.'

'No, no. You do not understand. That was just a joke – a good joke between me and Alice. She understood.'

'Funny kind of joke! Do you care to say where you were yesterday evening, Ascher?'

'Yes, yes – I tell you everything. I did not go near Alice. I am with friends – good friends. We are at the Seven Stars – and then we are at the Red Dog –'

He hurried on, his words stumbling over each other.

'Dick Willows – he was with me – and old Curdie – and George – and Platt and lots of the boys. I tell you I do not never go near Alice. Ach Gott, it is the truth I am telling you.'

His voice rose to a scream. The inspector nodded to his underling.

'Take him away. Detained on suspicion.'

'I don't know what to think,' he said as the unpleasant, shaking old man with the malevolent, mouthing jaw was removed. 'If it wasn't for the letter, I'd say he did it.'

'What about the men he mentions?'

'A bad crowd – not one of them would stick at perjury. I've no doubt he *was* with them the greater part of the evening. A lot depends on whether any one saw him near the shop between half-past five and six.'

Poirot shook his head thoughtfully.

'You are sure nothing was taken from the shop?'

The inspector shrugged his shoulders.

'That depends. A packet or two of cigarettes might have been taken – but you'd hardly commit murder for that.'

'And there was nothing – how shall I put it – introduced into the shop? Nothing that was odd there – incongruous?'

'There was a railway guide,' said the inspector.

'A railway guide?'

'Yes. It was open and turned face downward on the counter. Looked as though someone had been looking up the trains from Andover. Either the old woman or a customer.'

'Did she sell that type of thing?'

The inspector shook his head.

'She sold penny time-tables. This was a big one – kind of thing only Smith's or a big stationer would keep.'

A light came into Poirot's eyes. He leant forward.

A light came into the inspector's eye also.

'A railway guide, you say. A Bradshaw – *or an A B C?*'

'By the lord,' he said. 'It *was* an A B C.'

Chapter 5

Mary Drower

I think that I can date my interest in the case from that first mention of the A B C railway guide. Up till then I had not been able to raise much enthusiasm. This sordid murder of an old woman in a back-street shop was so like the usual type of crime reported in the newspapers that it failed to strike a significant note. In my own mind I had put down the anonymous letter with its mention of the 21st as a mere coincidence. Mrs Ascher, I felt reasonably sure, had been the victim of her drunken brute of a husband. But now the mention of the railway guide (so familiarly known by its abbreviation of A B C, listing as it did all railway stations in their alphabetical order) sent a quiver of excitement through me. Surely – surely this could not be a second coincidence?

The sordid crime took on a new aspect.

Who was the mysterious individual who had killed

Mrs Ascher and left an A B C railway guide behind him?

When we left the police station our first visit was to the mortuary to see the body of the dead woman. A strange feeling came over me as I gazed down on that wrinkled old face with the scanty grey hair drawn back tightly from the temples. It looked so peaceful, so incredibly remote from violence.

'Never knew who or what struck her,' observed the sergeant. 'That's what Dr Kerr says. I'm glad it was that way, poor old soul. A decent woman she was.'

'She must have been beautiful once,' said Poirot.

'Really?' I murmured incredulously.

'But yes, look at the line of the jaw, the bones, the moulding of the head.'

He sighed as he replaced the sheet and we left the mortuary.

Our next move was a brief interview with the police surgeon.

Dr Kerr was a competent-looking middle-aged man. He spoke briskly and with decision.

'The weapon wasn't found,' he said. 'Impossible to say what it may have been. A weighted stick, a club, a form of sandbag – any of those would fit the case.'

'Would much force be needed to strike such a blow?'

The doctor shot a keen glance at Poirot.

'Meaning, I suppose, could a shaky old man of

seventy do it? Oh, yes, it's perfectly possible – given sufficient weight in the head of the weapon, quite a feeble person could achieve the desired result.'

'Then the murderer could just as well be a woman as a man?'

The suggestion took the doctor somewhat aback.

'A woman, eh? Well, I confess it never occurred to me to connect a woman with this type of crime. But of course it's possible – perfectly possible. Only, psychologically speaking, I shouldn't say this was a woman's crime.'

Poirot nodded his head in eager agreement.

'Perfectly, perfectly. On the face of it, highly improbable. But one must take all possibilities into account. The body was lying – how?'

The doctor gave us a careful description of the position of the victim. It was his opinion that she had been standing with her back to the counter (and therefore to her assailant) when the blow had been struck. She had slipped down in a heap behind the counter quite out of sight of anyone entering the shop casually.

When we had thanked Dr Kerr and taken our leave, Poirot said:

'You perceive, Hastings, that we have already one further point in favour of Ascher's innocence. If he had been abusing his wife and threatening her, she would have been *facing* him over the counter. Instead she had her *back* to her assailant – obviously she is reaching down tobacco or cigarettes for a *customer*.'

I gave a little shiver.

'Pretty gruesome.'

Poirot shook his head gravely.

'*Pauvre femme*,' he murmured.

Then he glanced at his watch.

'Overton is not, I think, many miles from here. Shall we run over there and have an interview with the niece of the dead woman?'

'Surely you will go first to the shop where the crime took place?'

'I prefer to do that later. I have a reason.'

He did not explain further, and a few minutes later we were driving on the London road in the direction of Overton.

The address which the inspector had given us was that of a good-sized house about a mile on the London side of the village.

Our ring at the bell was answered by a pretty dark-haired girl whose eyes were red with recent weeping.

Poirot said gently:

'Ah! I think it is you who are Miss Mary Drower, the parlourmaid here?'

'Yes, sir, that's right. I'm Mary, sir.'

'Then perhaps I can talk to you for a few minutes

if your mistress will not object. It is about your aunt, Mrs Ascher.'

'The mistress is out, sir. She wouldn't mind, I'm sure, if you came in here.'

She opened the door of a small morning-room. We entered and Poirot, seating himself on a chair by the window, looked up keenly into the girl's face.

'You have heard of your aunt's death, of course?'

The girl nodded, tears coming once more into her eyes.

'This morning, sir. The police came over. Oh! it's terrible! Poor auntie! Such a hard life as she'd had, too. And now this – it's too awful.'

'The police did not suggest your returning to Andover?'

'They said I must come to the inquest – that's on Monday, sir. But I've nowhere to go there – I couldn't fancy being over the shop – now – and what with the housemaid being away, I didn't want to put the mistress out more than may be.'

'You were fond of your aunt, Mary?' said Poirot gently.

'Indeed I was, sir. Very good she's been to me always, auntie has. I went to her in London when I was eleven years old, after mother died. I started in service when I was sixteen, but I usually went along to auntie's on my day out. A lot of trouble she went through with that German fellow. "My old devil," she used to call him.

He'd never let her be in peace anywhere. Sponging, cadging old beast.'

The girl spoke with vehemence.

'Your aunt never thought of freeing herself by legal means from this persecution?'

'Well, you see, he was her husband, sir, you couldn't get away from that.'

The girl spoke simply but with finality.

'Tell me, Mary, he threatened her, did he not?'

'Oh, yes, sir, it was awful the things he used to say. That he'd cut her throat, and such like. Cursing and swearing too – both in German and in English. And yet auntie says he was a fine handsome figure of a man when she married him. It's dreadful to think, sir, what people come to.'

'Yes, indeed. And so, I suppose, Mary, having actually heard these threats, you were not so very surprised when you learnt what had happened?'

'Oh, but I was, sir. You see, sir, I never thought for one moment that he meant it. I thought it was just nasty talk and nothing more to it. And it isn't as though auntie was afraid of him. Why, I've seen him slink away like a dog with its tail between its legs when she turned on him. *He* was afraid of *her* if you like.'

'And yet she gave him money?'

'Well, he was her husband, you see, sir.'

'Yes, so you said before.' He paused for a minute or

two. Then he said: 'Suppose that, after all, he did *not* kill her.'

'Didn't kill her?'

She stared.

'That is what I said. Supposing someone else killed her . . . Have you any idea who that someone else could be?'

She stared at him with even more amazement.

'I've no idea, sir. It doesn't seem likely, though, does it?'

'There was no one your aunt was afraid of?'

Mary shook her head.

'Auntie wasn't afraid of people. She'd a sharp tongue and she'd stand up to anybody.'

'You never heard her mention anyone who had a grudge against her?'

'No, indeed, sir.'

'Did she ever get anonymous letters?'

'What kind of letters did you say, sir?'

'Letters that weren't signed – or only signed by something like A B C.' He watched her narrowly, but plainly she was at a loss. She shook her head wonderingly.

'Has your aunt any relations except you?'

'Not now, sir. One of ten she was, but only three lived to grow up. My Uncle Tom was killed in the war, and my Uncle Harry went to South America and no one's heard of him since, and mother's dead, of course, so there's only me.'

'Had your aunt any savings? Any money put by?'

'She'd a little in the Savings Bank, sir – enough to bury her proper, that's what she always said. Otherwise she didn't more than just make ends meet – what with her old devil and all.'

Poirot nodded thoughtfully. He said – perhaps more to himself than to her:

'At present one is in the dark – there is no direction – if things get clearer –' He got up. 'If I want you at any time, Mary, I will write to you here.'

'As a matter of fact, sir, I'm giving in my notice. I don't like the country. I stayed here because I fancied it was a comfort to auntie to have me near by. But now' – again the tears rose in her eyes – 'there's no reason I should stay, and so I'll go back to London. It's gayer for a girl there.'

'I wish that, when you do go, you would give me your address. Here is my card.'

He handed it to her. She looked at it with a puzzled frown.

'Then you're not – anything to do with the police, sir?'

'I am a private detective.'

She stood there looking at him for some moments in silence.

She said at last:

'Is there anything – queer going on, sir?'

'Yes, my child. There is – something queer going on. Later you may be able to help me.'

'I – I'll do anything, sir. It – it wasn't *right*, sir, auntie being killed.'

A strange way of putting it – but deeply moving.

A few seconds later we were driving back to Andover.

Chapter 6

The Scene of the Crime

The street in which the tragedy had occurred was a turning off the main street. Mrs Ascher's shop was situated about half-way down it on the right-hand side.

As we turned into the street Poirot glanced at his watch and I realized why he had delayed his visit to the scene of the crime until now. It was just on half-past five. He had wished to reproduce yesterday's atmosphere as closely as possible.

But if that had been his purpose it was defeated. Certainly at this moment the road bore very little likeness to its appearance on the previous evening. There were a certain number of small shops interspersed between private houses of the poorer class. I judged that ordinarily there would be a fair number of people passing up and down – mostly people of the poorer classes, with a good sprinkling of children playing on the pavements and in the road.

At this moment there was a solid mass of people standing staring at one particular house or shop and it took little perspicuity to guess which that was. What we saw was a mass of average human beings looking with intense interest at the spot where another human being had been done to death.

As we drew nearer this proved to be indeed the case. In front of a small dingy-looking shop with its shutters now closed stood a harassed-looking young policeman who was stolidly adjuring the crowd to 'pass along there.' By the help of a colleague, displacements took place – a certain number of people grudgingly sighed and betook themselves to their ordinary vocations, and almost immediately other persons came along and took up their stand to gaze their fill on the spot where murder had been committed.

Poirot stopped a little distance from the main body of the crowd. From where we stood the legend painted over the door could be read plainly enough. Poirot repeated it under his breath.

'A. Ascher. *Oui, c'est peut-être là –*'

He broke off.

'Come, let us go inside, Hastings.'

I was only too ready.

We made our way through the crowd and accosted the young policeman. Poirot produced the credentials which the inspector had given him. The constable nodded, and unlocked the door to let us pass within. We did so and entered to the intense interest of the lookers-on.

Inside it was very dark owing to the shutters being closed. The constable found and switched on the electric light. The bulb was a low-powered one so that the interior was still dimly lit.

I looked about me.

A dingy little place. A few cheap magazines strewn about, and yesterday's newspapers – all with a day's dust on them. Behind the counter a row of shelves reaching to the ceiling and packed with tobacco and packets of cigarettes. There were also a couple of jars of peppermint humbugs and barley sugar. A commonplace little shop, one of many thousand such others.

The constable in his slow Hampshire voice was explaining the *mise en scène*.

'Down in a heap behind the counter, that's where she was. Doctor says as how she never knew what hit her. Must have been reaching up to one of the shelves.'

'There was nothing in her hand?'

'No, sir, but there was a packet of Player's down beside her.'

Poirot nodded. His eyes swept round the small space observing – noting.

'And the railway guide was – where?'

'Here, sir.' The constable pointed out the spot on the

counter. 'It was open at the right page for Andover and lying face down. Seems as though he must have been looking up the trains to London. If so, it mightn't have been an Andover man at all. But then, of course, the railway guide might have belonged to someone else what had nothing to do with the murder at all, but just forgot it here.'

'Fingerprints?' I suggested.

The man shook his head.

'The whole place was examined straight away, sir. There weren't none.'

'Not on the counter itself?' asked Poirot.

'A long sight too many, sir! All confused and jumbled up.'

'Any of Ascher's among them?'

'Too soon to say, sir.'

Poirot nodded, then asked if the dead woman lived over the shop.

'Yes, sir, you go through that door at the back, sir. You'll excuse me not coming with you, but I've got to stay –'

Poirot passed through the door in question and I followed him. Behind the shop was a microscopic sort of parlour and kitchen combined – it was neat and clean but very dreary looking and scantily furnished. On the mantelpiece were a few photographs. I went up and looked at them and Poirot joined me.

The photographs were three in all. One was a cheap portrait of the girl we had been with that afternoon, Mary Drower. She was obviously wearing her best clothes and had the self-conscious, wooden smile on her face that so often disfigures the expression in posed photography, and makes a snapshot preferable.

The second was a more expensive type of picture – an artistically blurred reproduction of an elderly woman with white hair. A high fur collar stood up round the neck.

I guessed that this was probably the Miss Rose who had left Mrs Ascher the small legacy which had enabled her to start in business.

The third photograph was a very old one, now faded and yellow. It represented a young man and woman in somewhat old-fashioned clothes standing arm in arm. The man had a button-hole and there was an air of bygone festivity about the whole pose.

'Probably a wedding picture,' said Poirot. 'Regard, Hastings, did I not tell you that she had been a beautiful woman?'

He was right. Disfigured by old-fashioned hairdressing and weird clothes, there was no disguising the handsomeness of the girl in the picture with her clear-cut features and spirited bearing. I looked closely at the second figure. It was almost impossible to recognise the seedy Ascher in this smart young man with the military bearing.

I recalled the leering drunken old man, and the toil-worn face of the dead woman – and I shivered a little at the remorselessness of time . . .

From the parlour a stair led to two upstairs rooms. One was empty and unfurnished, the other had evidently been the dead woman's bedroom. After being searched by the police it had been left as it was. A couple of old worn blankets on the bed – a little stock of well-darned underwear in a drawer – cookery recipes in another – a paper-backed novel entitled *The Green Oasis* – a pair of new stockings – pathetic in their cheap shininess – a couple of china ornaments – a Dresden shepherd much broken, and a blue and yellow spotted dog – a black raincoat and a woolly jumper hanging on pegs – such were the worldly possessions of the late Alice Ascher.

If there had been any personal papers, the police had taken them.

'*Pauvre femme,*' murmured Poirot. 'Come, Hastings, there is nothing for us here.'

When we were once more in the street, he hesitated for a minute or two, then crossed the road. Almost exactly opposite Mrs Ascher's was a greengrocer's shop – of the type that has most of its stock outside rather than inside.

In a low voice Poirot gave me certain instructions. Then he himself entered the shop. After waiting a minute or two I followed him in. He was at the moment negotiating for a lettuce. I myself bought a pound of strawberries.

Poirot was talking animatedly to the stout lady who was serving him.

'It was just opposite you, was it not, that this murder occurred? What an affair! What a sensation it must have caused you!'

The stout lady was obviously tired of talking about the murder. She must have had a long day of it. She observed:

'It would be as well if some of that gaping crowd cleared off. What is there to look at, I'd like to know?'

'It must have been very different last night,' said Poirot. 'Possibly you even observed the murderer enter the shop – a tall, fair man with a beard, was he not? A Russian, so I have heard.'

'What's that?' The woman looked up sharply. 'A Russian did it, you say?'

'I understand that the police have arrested him.'

'Did you ever know?' The woman was excited, voluble. 'A foreigner.'

'*Mais oui*. I thought perhaps you might have noticed him last night?'

'Well, I don't get much chance of noticing, and that's a fact. The evening's our busy time and there's always a fair few passing along and getting home after their work. A tall, fair man with a beard – no, I can't say I saw anyone of that description anywhere about.'

I broke in on my cue.

'Excuse me, sir,' I said to Poirot. 'I think you have been misinformed. A short *dark* man I was told.'

An interested discussion intervened in which the stout lady, her lank husband and a hoarse-voiced shop-boy all participated. No less than four short dark men had been observed, and the hoarse boy had seen a tall fair one, 'but he hadn't got no beard,' he added regretfully.

Finally, our purchases made, we left the establishment, leaving our falsehoods uncorrected.

'And what was the point of all that, Poirot?' I demanded somewhat reproachfully.

'*Parbleu*, I wanted to estimate the chances of a stranger being noticed entering the shop opposite.'

'Couldn't you simply have asked – without all that tissue of lies?'

'No, *mon ami*. If I had "simply asked", as you put it, I should have got no answer at all to my questions. You yourself are English and yet you do not seem to appreciate the quality of the English reaction to a direct question. It is invariably one of suspicion and the natural result is reticence. If I had asked those people for information they would have shut up like oysters. But by making a statement (and a somewhat out of the way and preposterous one) and by your contradiction of it, tongues are immediately loosened. We know also that that particular time was a "busy time" – that is, that everyone would be intent on their own concerns and that there would be a fair number of people passing along the pavements. Our murderer chose his time well, Hastings.'

He paused and then added on a deep note of reproach:

'Is it that you have not in any degree the common sense, Hastings? I say to you: "Make a purchase *quelconque*" – and you deliberately choose the strawberries! Already they commence to creep through their bag and endanger your good suit.'

With some dismay, I perceived that this was indeed the case.

I hastily presented the strawberries to a small boy who seemed highly astonished and faintly suspicious.

Poirot added the lettuce, thus setting the seal on the child's bewilderment.

He continued to drive the moral home.

'At a cheap greengrocer's – *not* strawberries. A strawberry, unless fresh picked, is bound to exude juice. A banana – some apples – even a cabbage – but *strawberries* –'

'It was the first thing I thought of,' I explained by way of excuse.

'That is unworthy of your imagination,' returned Poirot sternly.

He paused on the sidewalk.

The house and shop on the right of Mrs Ascher's was empty. A 'To Let' sign appeared in the windows. On the other side was a house with somewhat grimy muslin curtains.

To this house Poirot betook himself and, there being no bell, executed a series of sharp flourishes with the knocker.

The door was opened after some delay by a very dirty child with a nose that needed attention.

'Good evening,' said Poirot. 'Is your mother within?'

'Ay?' said the child.

It stared at us with disfavour and deep suspicion.

'Your mother,' said Poirot.

This took some twelve seconds to sink in, then the child turned and, bawling up the stairs 'Mum, you're wanted,' retreated to some fastness in the dim interior.

A sharp-faced woman looked over the balusters and began to descend.

'No good you wasting your time –' she began, but Poirot interrupted her.

He took off his hat and bowed magnificently.

'Good evening, madame. I am on the staff of the *Evening Flicker*. I want to persuade you to accept a fee of five pounds and let us have an article on your late neighbour, Mrs Ascher.'

The irate words arrested on her lips, the woman came down the stairs smoothing her hair and hitching at her skirt.

'Come inside, please – on the left there. Won't you sit down, sir.'

The tiny room was heavily over-crowded with a massive pseudo-Jacobean suite, but we managed to squeeze ourselves in and on to a hard-seated sofa.

'You must excuse me,' the woman was saying. 'I am sure I'm sorry I spoke so sharp just now, but you'd hardly believe the worry one has to put up with – fellows coming along selling this, that and the other – vacuum cleaners, stockings, lavender bags and such-like foolery – and all so plausible and civil spoken. Got your name, too, pat they have. It's Mrs Fowler this, that and the other.'

Seizing adroitly on the name, Poirot said:

'Well, Mrs Fowler, I hope you're going to do what I ask.'

'I don't know, I'm sure.' The five pounds hung alluringly before Mrs Fowler's eyes. 'I *knew* Mrs Ascher, of course, but as to *writing* anything.'

Hastily Poirot reassured her. No labour on her part was required. He would elicit the facts from her and the interview would be written up.

Thus encouraged, Mrs Fowler plunged willingly into reminiscence, conjecture and hearsay.

Kept herself to herself, Mrs Ascher had. Not what you'd call really *friendly*, but there, she'd had a lot of trouble, poor soul, everyone knew that. And by rights Franz Ascher ought to have been locked up years ago. Not that Mrs Ascher had been afraid of him – real tartar she could be when roused! Give as good as she got any day. But there it was – the pitcher could go to the well once too often. Again and again, she, Mrs Fowler, had said to her: 'One of these days that man will do for you. Mark my words.' And he had done, hadn't he? And there had she, Mrs Fowler, been right next door and never heard a sound.

In a pause Poirot managed to insert a question.

Had Mrs Ascher ever received any peculiar letters – letters without a proper signature – just something like A B C?

Regretfully, Mrs Fowler returned a negative answer.

'I know the kind of thing you mean – anonymous letters they call them – mostly full of words you'd blush to say out loud. Well, I don't know, I'm sure, if Franz Ascher ever took to writing those. Mrs Ascher never let on to me if he did. What's that? A railway guide, an A B C? No, I never saw such a thing about – and I'm sure if Mrs Ascher had been sent one I'd have heard about it. I declare you could have knocked me down with a feather when I heard about this whole business. It was my girl Edie what came to me. "Mum," she says, "there's ever so many policemen next door." Gave me quite a turn, it did. "Well," I said, when I heard about it, "it does show that she ought never to have been alone in the house – that niece of hers ought to have been with her. A man in drink can be like a ravening wolf," I said, "and in my opinion a wild beast is neither more nor less than what that old devil of a husband of hers is. I've warned her," I said, "many times and now my words have come true. He'll do for you," I said. And he has done for her! You can't rightly estimate what a man will do when he's in drink and this murder's a proof of it.'

She wound up with a deep gasp.

'Nobody saw this man Ascher go into the shop, I believe?' said Poirot.

Mrs Fowler sniffed scornfully.

'Naturally he wasn't going to show himself,' she said.

How Mr Ascher had got there without showing himself she did not deign to explain.

She agreed that there was no back way into the house and that Ascher was quite well known by sight in the district.

'But he didn't want to swing for it and he kept himself well hid.'

Poirot kept the conversational ball rolling some little

time longer, but when it seemed certain that Mrs Fowler had told all that she knew not once but many times over, he terminated the interview, first paying out the promised sum.

'Rather a dear five pounds' worth, Poirot,' I ventured to remark when we were once more in the street.

'So far, yes.'

'You think she knows more than she has told?'

'My friend, we are in the peculiar position of *not knowing what questions to ask*. We are like little children playing *cache-cache* in the dark. We stretch out our hands and grope about. Mrs Fowler has told us all that she *thinks* she knows – and has thrown in several conjectures for good measure! In the future, however, her evidence may be useful. It is for the future that I have invested that sum of five pounds.'

I did not quite understand the point, but at this moment we ran into Inspector Glen.

Chapter 7

Mr Partridge and Mr Riddell

Inspector Glen was looking rather gloomy. He had, I gathered, spent the afternoon trying to get a complete list of persons who had been noticed entering the tobacco shop.

'And nobody has seen anyone?' Poirot inquired.

'Oh, yes, they have. Three tall men with furtive expressions – four short men with black moustaches – two beards – three fat men – all strangers – and all, if I'm to believe witnesses, with sinister expressions! I wonder somebody didn't see a gang of masked men with revolvers while they were about it!'

Poirot smiled sympathetically.

'Does anybody claim to have seen the man Ascher?'

'No, they don't. And that's another point in his favour. I've just told the Chief Constable that I think this is a job for Scotland Yard. I don't believe it's a local crime.'

Poirot said gravely:

'I agree with you.'

The inspector said:

'You know, Monsieur Poirot, it's a nasty business – a nasty business . . . I don't like it . . .'

We had two more interviews before returning to London.

The first was with Mr James Partridge. Mr Partridge was the last person known to have seen Mrs Ascher alive. He had made a purchase from her at 5.30.

Mr Partridge was a small man, a bank clerk by profession. He wore pince-nez, was very dry and spare-looking and extremely precise in all his utterances. He lived in a small house as neat and trim as himself.

'Mr – er – Poirot,' he said, glancing at the card my friend had handed to him. 'From Inspector Glen? What can I do for you, Mr Poirot?'

'I understand, Mr Partridge, that you were the last person to see Mrs Ascher alive.'

Mr Partridge placed his finger-tips together and looked at Poirot as though he were a doubtful cheque.

'That is a very debatable point, Mr Poirot,' he said. 'Many people may have made purchases from Mrs Ascher after I did so.'

'If so, they have not come forward to say so.'

Mr Partridge coughed.

'Some people, Mr Poirot, have no sense of public duty.'

He looked at us owlishly through his spectacles.

'Exceedingly true,' murmured Poirot. 'You, I understand, went to the police of your own accord?'

'Certainly I did. As soon as I heard of the shocking occurrence I perceived that my statement might be helpful and came forward accordingly.'

'A very proper spirit,' said Poirot solemnly. 'Perhaps you will be so kind as to repeat your story to me.'

'By all means. I was returning to this house and at 5.30 precisely –'

'Pardon, how was it that you knew the time so accurately?'

Mr Partridge looked a little annoyed at being interrupted.

'The church clock chimed. I looked at my watch and found I was a minute slow. That was just before I entered Mrs Ascher's shop.'

'Were you in the habit of making purchases there?'

'Fairly frequently. It was on my way home. About once or twice a week I was in the habit of purchasing two ounces of John Cotton mild.'

'Did you know Mrs Ascher at all? Anything of her circumstances or her history?'

'Nothing whatever. Beyond my purchase and an

occasional remark as to the state of the weather, I had never spoken to her.'

'Did you know she had a drunken husband who was in the habit of threatening her life?'

'No, I knew nothing whatever about her.'

'You knew her by sight, however. Did anything about her appearance strike you as unusual yesterday evening? Did she appear flurried or put out in any way?'

Mr Partridge considered.

'As far as I noticed, she seemed exactly as usual,' he said.

Poirot rose.

'Thank you, Mr Partridge, for answering these questions. Have you, by any chance, an A B C in the house? I want to look up my return train to London.'

'On the shelf just behind you,' said Mr Partridge.

On the shelf in question were an A B C, a Bradshaw, the Stock Exchange Year Book, Kelly's Directory, a Who's Who and a local directory.

Poirot took down the A B C, pretended to look up a train, then thanked Mr Partridge and took his leave.

Our next interview was with Mr Albert Riddell and was of a highly different character. Mr Albert Riddell was a platelayer and our conversation took place to the accompaniment of the clattering of plates and dishes by Mr Riddell's obviously nervous wife, the growling of Mr Riddell's dog and the undisguised hostility of Mr Riddell himself.

He was a big clumsy giant of a man with a broad face and small suspicious eyes. He was in the act of eating meat-pie, washed down by exceedingly black tea. He peered at us angrily over the rim of his cup.

'Told all I've got to tell once, haven't I?' he growled. 'What's it to do with me, anyway? Told it to the blarsted police, I 'ave, and now I've got to spit it all out again to a couple of blarsted foreigners.'

Poirot gave a quick, amused glance in my direction and then said:

'In truth I sympathize with you, but what will you? It is a question of murder, is it not? One has to be very, very careful.'

'Best tell the gentleman what he wants, Bert,' said the woman nervously.

'You shut your blarsted mouth,' roared the giant.

'You did not, I think, go to the police of your own accord.' Poirot slipped the remark in neatly.

'Why the hell should I? It were no business of mine.'

'A matter of opinion,' said Poirot indifferently. 'There has been a murder – the police want to know who has been in the shop – I myself think it would have – what shall I say? – looked more natural if you had come forward.'

'I've got my work to do. Don't say I shouldn't have come forward in my own time –'

'But as it was, the police were given your name as that of a person seen to go into Mrs Ascher's and they had to come to you. Were they satisfied with your account?'

'Why shouldn't they be?' demanded Bert truculently.

Poirot merely shrugged his shoulders.

'What are you getting at, mister? Nobody's got anything against me? Everyone knows who did the old girl in, that b – of a husband of hers.'

'But he was not in the street that evening and you were.'

'Trying to fasten it on me, are you? Well, you won't succeed. What reason had I got to do a thing like that? Think I wanted to pinch a tin of her bloody tobacco? Think I'm a bloody homicidal maniac as they call it? Think I –?'

He rose threateningly from his seat. His wife bleated out:

'Bert, Bert – don't say such things. Bert – they'll think –'

'Calm yourself, monsieur,' said Poirot. 'I demand only your account of your visit. That you refuse it seems to me – what shall we say – a little odd?'

'Who said I refused anything?' Mr Riddell sank back again into his seat. 'I don't mind.'

'It was six o'clock when you entered the shop?'

'That's right – a minute or two after, as a matter of fact. Wanted a packet of Gold Flake. I pushed open the door –'

'It was closed, then?'

'That's right. I thought shop was shut, maybe. But it wasn't. I went in, there wasn't anyone about. I hammered on the counter and waited a bit. Nobody came, so I went out again. That's all, and you can put it in your pipe and smoke it.'

'You didn't see the body fallen down behind the counter?'

'No, no more would you have done – unless you was looking for it, maybe.'

'Was there a railway guide lying about?'

'Yes, there was – face downwards. It crossed my mind like that the old woman might have had to go off sudden by train and forgot to lock shop up.'

'Perhaps you picked up the railway guide or moved it along the counter?'

'Didn't touch the b – thing. I did just what I said.'

'And you did not see anyone leaving the shop before you yourself got there?'

'Didn't see any such thing. What I say is, why pitch on me –?'

Poirot rose.

'Nobody is pitching upon you – yet. Bonsoir, monsieur.'

He left the man with his mouth open and I followed him.

In the street he consulted his watch.

'With great haste, my friend, we might manage to catch the 7.2. Let us despatch ourselves quickly.'

Chapter 8

The Second Letter

'Well?' I demanded eagerly.

We were seated in a first-class carriage which we had to ourselves. The train, an express, had just drawn out of Andover.

'The crime,' said Poirot, 'was committed by a man of medium height with red hair and a cast in the left eye. He limps slightly on the right foot and has a mole just below the shoulder-blade.'

'Poirot?' I cried.

For the moment I was completely taken in. Then the twinkle in my friend's eye undeceived me.

'Poirot!' I said again, this time in reproach.

'*Mon ami*, what will you? You fix upon me a look of doglike devotion and demand of me a pronouncement à la Sherlock Holmes! Now for the truth – *I do not know what the murderer looks like, nor where he lives, nor how to set hands upon him.*'

'If only he had left some clue,' I murmured.

'Yes, the clue – it is always the clue that attracts you. Alas that he did not smoke the cigarette and leave the ash, and then step in it with a shoe that has nails of a curious pattern. No – he is not so obliging. But at least, my friend, you have the *railway guide*. The A B C, that is a clue for you!'

'Do you think he left it by mistake then?'

'Of course not. He left it on purpose. The fingerprints tell us that.'

'But there weren't any on it.'

'That is what I mean. What was yesterday evening? A warm June night. Does a man stroll about on such an evening in *gloves*? Such a man would certainly have attracted attention. Therefore since there are no fingerprints on the A B C, it must have been carefully wiped. An innocent man would have left prints – a guilty man would not. So our murderer left it there for a purpose – but for all that it is none the less a clue. That A B C was bought by someone – it was carried by someone – there is a possibility there.'

'You think we may learn something that way?'

'Frankly, Hastings, I am not particularly hopeful. This man, this unknown X, obviously prides himself on his abilities. He is not likely to blaze a trail that can be followed straight away.'

'So that really the ABC isn't helpful at all.'

'Not in the sense you mean.'

'In any sense?'

Poirot did not answer at once. Then he said slowly:

'The answer to that is yes. We are confronted here by an unknown personage. He is in the dark and seeks to remain in the dark. But in the very nature of things *he cannot help throwing light upon himself*. In one sense we know nothing about him – in another sense we know already a good deal. I see his figure dimly taking shape – a man who prints clearly and well – who buys good-quality paper – who is at great needs to express his personality. I see him as a child possibly ignored and passed over – I see him growing up with an inward sense of inferiority – warring with a sense of injustice . . . I see that inner urge – to assert himself – to focus attention on himself ever becoming stronger, and events, circumstances – crushing it down – heaping, perhaps, more humiliations on him. And inwardly the match is set to the powder train . . .'

'That's all pure conjecture,' I objected. 'It doesn't give you any practical help.'

'You prefer the match end, the cigarette ash, the nailed boots! You always have. But at least we can ask ourselves some practical questions. Why the A B C? Why Mrs Ascher? Why Andover?'

'The woman's past life seems simple enough,' I

mused. 'The interviews with those two men were disappointing. They couldn't tell us anything more than we knew already.'

'To tell the truth, I did not expect much in that line. But we could not neglect two possible candidates for the murder.'

'Surely you don't think –'

'There is at least a possibility that the murderer lives in or near Andover. That is a possible answer to our question: "Why Andover?" Well, here were two men known to have been in the shop at the requisite time of day. Either of them *might* be the murderer. And there is nothing as yet to show that one or other of them is *not* the murderer.'

'That great hulking brute, Riddell, perhaps,' I admitted.

'Oh, I am inclined to acquit Riddell off-hand. He was nervous, blustering, obviously uneasy –'

'But surely that just shows –'

'A nature diametrically opposed to that which penned the A B C letter. Conceit and self-confidence are the characteristics that we must look for.'

'Someone who throws his weight about?'

'Possibly. But some people, under a nervous and self-effacing manner, conceal a great deal of vanity and self-satisfaction.'

'You don't think that little Mr Partridge –'

'He is more *le type*. One cannot say more than that. He acts as the writer of the letter would act – goes at once to the police – pushes himself to the fore – enjoys his position.'

'Do you really think –?'

'No, Hastings. Personally I believe that the murderer came from outside Andover, but we must neglect no avenue of research. And although I say "he" all the time, we must not exclude the possibility of a woman being concerned.'

'Surely not!'

'The method of attack is that of a man, I agree. But anonymous letters are written by women rather than by men. We must bear that in mind.'

I was silent for a few minutes, then I said:

'What do we do next?'

'My energetic Hastings,' Poirot said and smiled at me.

'No, but what do we do?'

'Nothing.'

'Nothing?' My disappointment rang out clearly.

'Am I the magician? The sorcerer? What would you have me do?'

Turning the matter over in my mind I found it difficult to give an answer. Nevertheless I felt convinced that something ought to be done and that we should not allow the grass to grow under our feet.

I said:

'There is the A B C – and the notepaper and envelope –'

'Naturally everything is being done in that line. The police have all the means at their disposal for that kind of inquiry. If anything is to be discovered on those lines have no fear but that they will discover it.'

With that I was forced to rest content.

In the days that followed I found Poirot curiously disinclined to discuss the case. When I tried to reopen the subject he waved it aside with an impatient hand.

In my own mind I was afraid that I fathomed his motive. Over the murder of Mrs Ascher, Poirot had sustained a defeat. A B C had challenged him – and A B C had won. My friend, accustomed to an unbroken line of successes, was sensitive to his failure – so much so that he could not even endure discussion of the subject. It was, perhaps, a sign of pettiness in so great a man, but even the most sober of us is liable to have his head turned by success. In Poirot's case the head-turning process had been going on for years. Small wonder if its effects became noticeable at long last.

Understanding, I respected my friend's weakness and I made no further reference to the case. I read in the paper the account of the inquest. It was very brief, no mention was made of the A B C letter, and a verdict was returned of murder by some person or persons unknown. The crime attracted very little attention in the press. It had no popular or spectacular features. The murder of an old woman in a side street was soon passed over in the press for more thrilling topics.

Truth to tell, the affair was fading from my mind also, partly, I think, because I disliked to think of Poirot as being in any way associated with a failure, when on July 25th it was suddenly revived.

I had not seen Poirot for a couple of days as I had been away in Yorkshire for the weekend. I arrived back on Monday afternoon and the letter came by the six o'clock post. I remember the sudden, sharp intake of breath that Poirot gave as he slit open that particular envelope.

'It has come,' he said.

I stared at him – not understanding.

'What has come?'

'The second chapter of the A B C business.'

For a minute I looked at him uncomprehendingly. The matter had really passed from my memory.

'Read,' said Poirot and passed me over the letter.

As before, it was printed on good-quality paper.

Dear Mr Poirot, – Well, what about it? First game to me, I think. The Andover business went with a swing, didn't it?

But the fun's only just beginning. Let me draw your attention to Bexhill-on-Sea. Date, the 25th inst.

What a merry time we are having! Yours etc.

A B C

'Good God, Poirot,' I cried. 'Does this mean that this fiend is going to attempt another crime?'

'Naturally, Hastings. What else did you expect? Did you think that the Andover business was an isolated case? Do you not remember my saying: "This is the beginning"?'

'But this is horrible!'

'Yes, it is horrible.'

'We're up against a homicidal maniac.'

'Yes.'

His quietness was more impressive than any heroics could have been. I handed back the letter with a shudder.

The following morning saw us at a conference of powers. The Chief Constable of Sussex, the Assistant Commissioner of the CID, Inspector Glen from Andover, Superintendent Carter of the Sussex police, Japp and a younger inspector called Crome, and Dr Thompson, the famous alienist, were all assembled together. The postmark on this letter was Hampstead, but in Poirot's opinion little importance could be attached to this fact.

The matter was discussed fully. Dr Thompson was a pleasant middle-aged man who, in spite of his learning, contented himself with homely language, avoiding the technicalities of his profession.

'There's no doubt,' said the Assistant Commissioner, 'that the two letters are in the same hand. Both were written by the same person.'

'And we can fairly assume that that person was responsible for the Andover murder.'

'Quite. We've now got definite warning of a second crime scheduled to take place on the 25th – the day after tomorrow – at Bexhill. What steps can be taken?'

The Sussex Chief Constable looked at his superintendent.

'Well, Carter, what about it?'

The superintendent shook his head gravely.

'It's difficult, sir. There's not the least clue towards whom the victim may be. Speaking fair and square, what steps *can* we take?'

'A suggestion,' murmured Poirot.

Their faces turned to him.

'I think it possible that the surname of the intended victim will begin with the letter B.'

'That would be something,' said the superintendent doubtfully.

'An alphabetical complex,' said Dr Thompson thoughtfully.

'I suggest it as a possibility – no more. It came into my mind when I saw the name Ascher clearly written over the shop door of the unfortunate woman who was murdered last month. When I got the letter naming Bexhill it occurred to me as a possibility that the victim as well as the place might be selected by an alphabetical system.'

'It's possible,' said the doctor. 'On the other hand, it may be that the name Ascher was a coincidence – that the victim this time, no matter what her name is, will again be an old woman who keeps a shop. We're dealing, remember, with a madman. So far he hasn't given us any clue as to motive.'

'Has a madman any motive, sir?' asked the superintendent sceptically.

'Of course he has, man. A deadly logic is one of the special characteristics of acute mania. A man may believe himself divinely appointed to kill clergymen – or doctors – or old women in tobacco shops – and there's always some perfectly coherent reason behind it. We mustn't let the alphabetical business run away with us. Bexhill succeeding to Andover *may* be a mere coincidence.'

'We can at least take certain precautions, Carter, and make a special note of the B's, especially small shopkeepers, and keep a watch on all small tobacconists and newsagents looked after by a single person. I don't think there's anything more we can do than that. Naturally, keep tabs on all strangers as far as possible.'

The superintendent uttered a groan.

'With the schools breaking up and the holidays beginning? People are fairly flooding into the place this week.'

'We must do what we can,' the Chief Constable said sharply.

Inspector Glen spoke in his turn.

'I'll have a watch kept on anyone connected with the Ascher business. Those two witnesses, Partridge and Riddell, and of course Ascher himself. If they show any sign of leaving Andover they'll be followed.'

The conference broke up after a few more suggestions and a little desultory conversation.

'Poirot,' I said as we walked along by the river. 'Surely this crime can be prevented?'

He turned a haggard face to me.

'The sanity of a city full of men against the insanity of one man? I fear, Hastings – I very much fear. Remember the long-continued successes of Jack the Ripper.'

'It's horrible,' I said.

'Madness, Hastings, is a terrible thing . . . *I am afraid . . . I am very much afraid . . .*'

Chapter 9

The Bexhill-on-Sea Murder

I still remember my awakening on the morning of the 25th of July. It must have been about seven-thirty.

Poirot was standing by my bedside gently shaking me by the shoulder. One glance at his face brought me from semi-consciousness into the full possession of my faculties.

'What is it?' I demanded, sitting up rapidly.

His answer came quite simply, but a wealth of emotion lay behind the three words he uttered.

'*It has happened.*'

'What?' I cried. 'You mean – but *today* is the 25th.'

'It took place last night – or rather in the early hours of this morning.'

As I sprang from bed and made a rapid toilet, he recounted briefly what he had just learnt over the telephone.

'The body of a young girl has been found on the

beach at Bexhill. She has been identified as Elizabeth Barnard, a waitress in one of the cafés, who lived with her parents in a little recently built bungalow. Medical evidence gave the time of death as between 11.30 and 1 am.'

'They're quite sure that this is *the* crime?' I asked, as I hastily lathered my face.

'*An ABC open at the trains to Bexhill was found actually under the body*.'

I shivered.

'This is horrible!'

'*Faites attention*, Hastings. I do not want a second tragedy in my rooms!'

I wiped the blood from my chin rather ruefully.

'What is our plan of campaign?' I asked.

'The car will call for us in a few moments' time. I will bring you a cup of coffee here so that there will be no delay in starting.'

Twenty minutes later we were in a fast police car crossing the Thames on our way out of London.

With us was Inspector Crome, who had been present at the conference the other day, and who was officially in charge of the case.

Crome was a very different type of officer from Japp. A much younger man, he was the silent, superior type. Well educated and well read, he was, for my taste, several shades too pleased with himself. He had lately gained kudos over a series of child murders, having patiently tracked down the criminal who was now in Broadmoor.

He was obviously a suitable person to undertake the present case, but I thought that he was just a little too aware of the fact himself. His manner to Poirot was a shade patronising. He deferred to him as a younger man to an older one – in a rather self-conscious, 'public school' way.

'I've had a good long talk with Dr Thompson,' he said. 'He's very interested in the "chain" or "series" type of murder. It's the product of a particular distorted type of mentality. As a layman one can't, of course, appreciate the finer points as they present themselves to a medical point of view.' He coughed. 'As a matter of fact – my last case – I don't know whether you read about it – the Mabel Homer case, the Muswell Hill schoolgirl, you know – that man Capper was extraordinary. Amazingly difficult to pin the crime on to him – it was his third, too! Looked as sane as you or I. But there are various tests – verbal traps, you know – quite modern, of course, there was nothing of that kind in your day. Once you can induce a man to give himself away, you've got him! He knows that you know and his nerve goes. He starts giving himself away right and left.'

'Even in my day that happened sometimes,' said Poirot.

Inspector Crome looked at him and murmured conversationally:

'Oh, yes?'

There was silence between us for some time. As we passed New Cross Station, Crome said:

'If there's anything you want to ask me about the case, pray do so.'

'You have not, I presume, a description of the dead girl?'

'She was twenty-three years of age, engaged as a waitress at the Ginger Cat café –'

'*Pas ça*. I wondered – if she were pretty?'

'As to that I've no information,' said Inspector Crome with a hint of withdrawal. His manner said: 'Really – these foreigners! All the same!'

A faint look of amusement came into Poirot's eyes.

'It does not seem to you important, that? Yet, *pour une femme*, it is of the first importance. Often it decides her destiny!'

Another silence fell.

It was not until we were nearing Sevenoaks that Poirot opened the conversation again.

'Were you informed, by any chance, how and with what the girl was strangled?'

Inspector Crome replied briefly.

'Strangled with her own belt – a thick, knitted affair, I gather.'

Poirot's eyes opened very wide.

'Aha,' he said. 'At last we have a piece of information that is very definite. That tells one something, does it not?'

'I haven't seen it yet,' said Inspector Crome coldly.

I felt impatient with the man's caution and lack of imagination.

'It gives us the hallmark of the murderer,' I said. 'The girl's own belt. It shows the particular beastliness of his mind!'

Poirot shot me a glance I could not fathom. On the face of it it conveyed humorous impatience. I thought that perhaps it was a warning not to be too outspoken in front of the inspector.

I relapsed into silence.

At Bexhill we were greeted by Superintendent Carter. He had with him a pleasant-faced, intelligent-looking young inspector called Kelsey. The latter was detailed to work in with Crome over the case.

'You'll want to make your own inquiries, Crome,' said the superintendent. 'So I'll just give you the main heads of the matter and then you can get busy right away.'

'Thank you, sir,' said Crome.

'We've broken the news to her father and mother,' said the superintendent. 'Terrible shock to them, of course. I left them to recover a bit before questioning them, so you can start from the beginning there.'

'There are other members of the family – yes?' asked Poirot.

'There's a sister – a typist in London. She's been communicated with. And there's a young man – in fact, the girl was supposed to be out with him last night, I gather.'

'Any help from the A B C guide?' asked Crome.

'It's there,' the superintendent nodded towards the table. 'No fingerprints. Open at the page for Bexhill. A new copy, I should say – doesn't seem to have been opened much. Not bought anywhere round here. I've tried all the likely stationers.'

'Who discovered the body, sir?'

'One of these fresh-air, early-morning colonels. Colonel Jerome. He was out with his dog about 6 am. Went along the front in the direction of Cooden, and down on to the beach. Dog went off and sniffed at something. Colonel called it. Dog didn't come. Colonel had a look and thought something queer was up. Went over and looked. Behaved very properly. Didn't touch her at all and rang us up immediately.'

'And the time of death was round about midnight last night?'

'Between midnight and 1 am – that's pretty certain. Our homicidal joker is a man of his word. If he says the 25th, it is the 25th – though it may have been only by a few minutes.'

Crome nodded.

'Yes, that's his mentality all right. There's nothing else? Nobody saw anything helpful?'

'Not as far as we know. But it's early yet. Everyone who saw a girl in white walking with a man last night will be along to tell us about it soon, and as I imagine there were about four or five hundred girls in white walking with young men last night, it ought to be a nice business.'

'Well, sir, I'd better get down to it,' said Crome. 'There's the café and there's the girl's home. I'd better go to both of them. Kelsey can come with me.'

'And Mr Poirot?' asked the superintendent.

'I will accompany you,' said Poirot to Crome with a little bow.

Crome, I thought, looked slightly annoyed. Kelsey, who had not seen Poirot before, grinned broadly.

It was an unfortunate circumstance that the first time people saw my friend they were always disposed to consider him as a joke of the first water.

'What about this belt she was strangled with?' asked Crome. 'Mr Poirot is inclined to think it's a valuable clue. I expect he'd like to see it.'

'*Du tout*,' said Poirot quickly. 'You misunderstood me.'

'You'll get nothing from that,' said Carter. 'It wasn't a leather belt – might have got fingerprints if it had been. Just a thick sort of knitted silk – ideal for the purpose.'

I gave a shiver.

'Well,' said Crome, 'we'd better be getting along.'

We set out forthwith.

Our first visit was to the Ginger Cat. Situated on the sea front, this was the usual type of small tearoom. It had little tables covered with orange-checked cloths and basket-work chairs of exceeding discomfort with orange cushions on them. It was the kind of place that specialized in morning coffee, five different kinds of teas (Devonshire, Farmhouse, Fruit, Carlton and Plain), and a few sparing lunch dishes for females such as scrambled eggs and shrimps and macaroni au gratin.

The morning coffees were just getting under way. The manageress ushered us hastily into a very untidy back sanctum.

'Miss – eh – Merrion?' inquired Crome.

Miss Merrion bleated out in a high, distressed-gentlewoman voice:

'That is my name. This is a most distressing business. Most distressing. How it will affect our business I really cannot *think*!'

Miss Merrion was a very thin woman of forty with wispy orange hair (indeed she was astonishingly like a ginger cat herself). She played nervously with various fichus and frills that were part of her official costume.

'You'll have a boom,' said Inspector Kelsey encouragingly. 'You'll see! You won't be able to serve teas fast enough!'

'Disgusting,' said Miss Merrion. 'Truly disgusting. It makes one despair of human nature.'

But her eyes brightened nevertheless.

'What can you tell me about the dead girl, Miss Merrion?'

'Nothing,' said Miss Merrion positively. 'Absolutely nothing!'

'How long had she been working here?'

'This was the second summer.'

'You were satisfied with her?'

'She was a good waitress – quick and obliging.'

'She was pretty, yes?' inquired Poirot.

Miss Merrion, in her turn, gave him an 'Oh, these foreigners' look.

'She was a nice, clean-looking girl,' she said distantly.

'What time did she go off duty last night?' asked Crome.

'Eight o'clock. We close at eight. We do not serve dinners. There is no demand for them. Scrambled eggs and tea (Poirot shuddered) people come in for up to seven o'clock and sometimes after, but our rush is over by 6.30.'

'Did she mention to you how she proposed to spend her evening?'

'Certainly not,' said Miss Merrion emphatically. 'We were not on those terms.'

'No one came in and called for her? Anything like that?'

'No.'

'Did she seem quite her ordinary self? Not excited or depressed?'

'Really I could not say,' said Miss Merrion aloofly.

'How many waitresses do you employ?'

'Two normally, and an extra two after the 20th July until the end of August.'

'But Elizabeth Barnard was not one of the extras?'

'Miss Barnard was one of the regulars.'

'What about the other one?'

'Miss Higley? She is a very nice young lady.'

'Were she and Miss Barnard friends?'

'Really I could not say.'

'Perhaps we'd better have a word with her.'

'Now?'

'If you please.'

'I will send her to you,' said Miss Merrion, rising. 'Please keep her as short a time as possible. This is the morning coffee rush hour.'

The feline and gingery Miss Merrion left the room.

'Very refined,' remarked Inspector Kelsey. He mimicked the lady's mincing tone. *'Really I could not say.'*

A plump girl, slightly out of breath, with dark hair, rosy cheeks and dark eyes goggling with excitement, bounced in.

'Miss Merrion sent me,' she announced breathlessly.

'Miss Higley?'

'Yes, that's me.'

'You knew Elizabeth Barnard?'

'Oh, yes, I knew Betty. Isn't it *awful*? It's just too awful! I can't believe it's true. I've been saying to the girls all the morning I just *can't* believe it! "You know, girls," I said, "it just doesn't seem *real.* Betty! I mean, Betty Barnard, who's been here all along, *murdered*! I just can't believe it," I said. Five or six times I've pinched myself just to see if I wouldn't wake up. Betty murdered . . . It's – well, you know what I mean – it doesn't seem *real.*'

'You knew the dead girl well?' asked Crome.

'Well, she's worked here longer than I have. I only came this March. She was here last year. She was rather quiet, if you know what I mean. She wasn't one to joke or laugh a lot. I don't mean that she was exactly *quiet* – she'd plenty of fun in her and all that – but she didn't – well, she was quiet and she wasn't quiet, if you know what I mean.'

I will say for Inspector Crome that he was exceedingly patient. As a witness the buxom Miss Higley was persistently maddening. Every statement she made was repeated and qualified half a dozen times. The net result was meagre in the extreme.

She had not been on terms of intimacy with the dead girl. Elizabeth Barnard, it could be guessed, had considered herself a cut above Miss Higley. She had been friendly in working hours, but the girls had not seen much of her out of them. Elizabeth Barnard had had a 'friend' who worked at the estate agents near the station. Court & Brunskill. No, he wasn't Mr Court nor Mr Brunskill. He was a clerk there. She didn't know his name. But she knew him by sight well. Good-looking – oh, very good-looking, and always so nicely dressed. Clearly, there was a tinge of jealousy in Miss Higley's heart.

In the end it boiled down to this. Elizabeth Barnard had not confided in anyone in the café as to her plans for the evening, but in Miss Higley's opinion she had been going to meet her 'friend'. She had had on a new white dress, 'ever so sweet with one of the new necks.'

We had a word with each of the other two girls but with no further results. Betty Barnard had not said anything as to her plans and no one had noticed her in Bexhill during the course of the evening.

Chapter 10

The Barnards

Elizabeth Barnard's parents lived in a minute bungalow, one of fifty or so recently run up by a speculative builder on the confines of the town. The name of it was Llandudno. Mr Barnard, a stout, bewildered-looking man of fifty-five or so, had noticed our approach and was standing waiting in the doorway.

'Come in, gentlemen,' he said.

Inspector Kelsey took the initiative.

'This is Inspector Crome of Scotland Yard, sir,' he said. 'He's come down to help us over this business.'

'Scotland Yard?' said Mr Barnard hopefully. 'That's good. This murdering villain's got to be laid by the heels. My poor little girl –' His face was distorted by a spasm of grief.

'And this is Mr Hercule Poirot, also from London, and er –'

'Captain Hastings,' said Poirot.

'Pleased to meet you, gentlemen,' said Mr Barnard mechanically. 'Come into the snuggery. I don't know that my poor wife's up to seeing you. All broken up, she is.'

However, by the time that we were ensconced in the living room of the bungalow, Mrs Barnard had made her appearance. She had evidently been crying bitterly, her eyes were reddened and she walked with the uncertain gait of a person who had had a great shock.

'Why, mother, that's fine,' said Mr Barnard. 'You're sure you're all right – eh?'

He patted her shoulder and drew her down into a chair.

'The superintendent was very kind,' said Mr Barnard. 'After he'd broken the news to us, he said he'd leave any questions till later when we'd got over the first shock.'

'It is too cruel. Oh, it is too cruel,' cried Mrs Barnard tearfully. 'The cruellest thing that ever was, it is.'

Her voice had a faintly sing-song intonation that I thought for a moment was foreign till I remembered the name on the gate and realized that the 'effer wass' of her speech was in reality proof of her Welsh origin.

'It's very painful, madam, I know,' said Inspector Crome. 'And we've every sympathy for you, but we want to know all the facts we can so as to get to work as quick as possible.'

'That's sense, that is,' said Mr Barnard, nodding approval.

'Your daughter was twenty-three, I understand. She lived here with you and worked at the Ginger Cat café, is that right?'

'That's it.'

'This is a new place, isn't it? Where did you live before?'

'I was in the ironmongery business in Kennington. Retired two years ago. Always meant to live near the sea.'

'You have two daughters?'

'Yes. My elder daughter works in an office in London.'

'Weren't you alarmed when your daughter didn't come home last night?'

'We didn't know she hadn't,' said Mrs Barnard tearfully. 'Dad and I always go to bed early. Nine o'clock's our time. We never knew Betty hadn't come home till the police officer came and said – and said –'

She broke down.

'Was your daughter in the habit of – er – returning home late?'

'You know what girls are nowadays, inspector,' said Barnard. 'Independent, that's what they are. These summer evenings they're not going to rush home. All the same, Betty was usually in by eleven.'

'How did she get in? Was the door open?'

'Left the key under the mat – that's what we always did.'

'There is some rumour, I believe, that your daughter was engaged to be married?'

'They don't put it as formally as that nowadays,' said Mr Barnard.

'Donald Fraser his name is, and I liked him. I liked him very much,' said Mrs Barnard. 'Poor fellow, it'll be trouble for him – this news. Does he know yet, I wonder?'

'He works in Court & Brunskill's, I understand?'

'Yes, they're the estate agents.'

'Was he in the habit of meeting your daughter most evenings after her work?'

'Not every evening. Once or twice a week would be nearer.'

'Do you know if she was going to meet him yesterday?'

'She didn't say. Betty never said much about what she was doing or where she was going. But she was a good girl, Betty was. Oh, I can't believe –'

Mrs Barnard started sobbing again.

'Pull yourself together, old lady. Try to hold up, mother,' urged her husband. 'We've got to get to the bottom of this.'

'I'm sure Donald would never – would never –' sobbed Mrs Barnard.

'Now just you pull yourself together,' repeated Mr Barnard.

'I wish to God I could give you some help – but the plain fact is I know nothing – nothing at all that can help you to find the dastardly scoundrel who did this. Betty was just a merry, happy girl – with a decent young fellow that she was – well, we'd have called it walking out with in my young days. Why anyone should want to murder her simply beats me – it doesn't make sense.'

'You're very near the truth there, Mr Barnard,' said Crome. 'I tell you what I'd like to do – have a look over Miss Barnard's room. There may be something – letters – or a diary.'

'Look over it and welcome,' said Mr Barnard, rising.

He led the way. Crome followed him, then Poirot, then Kelsey, and I brought up the rear.

I stopped for a minute to retie my shoelaces, and as I did so a taxi drew up outside and a girl jumped out of it. She paid the driver and hurried up the path to the house, carrying a small suitcase. As she entered the door she saw me and stopped dead.

There was something so arresting in her pose that it intrigued me.

'Who are you?' she said.

I came down a few steps. I felt embarrassed as to how exactly to reply. Should I give my name? Or mention that I had come here with the police? The girl, however, gave me no time to make a decision.

'Oh, well,' she said, 'I can guess.'

She pulled off the little white woollen cap she was wearing and threw it on the ground. I could see her better now as she turned a little so that the light fell on her.

My first impression was of the Dutch dolls that my sisters used to play with in my childhood. Her hair was black and cut in a straight bob and a bang across the forehead. Her cheek-bones were high and her whole figure had a queer modern angularity that was not, somehow, unattractive. She was not good-looking – plain rather – but there was an intensity about her, a forcefulness that made her a person quite impossible to overlook.

'You are Miss Barnard?' I asked.

'I am Megan Barnard. You belong to the police, I suppose?'

'Well,' I said. 'Not exactly –'

She interrupted me.

'I don't think I've got anything to say to you. My sister was a nice bright girl with no men friends. Good morning.'

She gave me a short laugh as she spoke and regarded me challengingly.

'That's the correct phrase, I believe?' she said.

'I'm not a reporter, if that's what you're getting at.'

'Well, what are you?' She looked around. 'Where's mum and dad?'

'Your father is showing the police your sister's bedroom. Your mother's in there. She's very upset.'

The girl seemed to make a decision.

'Come in here,' she said.

She pulled open a door and passed through. I followed her and found myself in a small, neat kitchen.

I was about to shut the door behind me – but found an unexpected resistance. The next moment Poirot had slipped quietly into the room and shut the door behind him.

'Mademoiselle Barnard?' he said with a quick bow.

'This is M. Hercule Poirot,' I said.

Megan Barnard gave him a quick, appraising glance.

'I've heard of you,' she said. 'You're the fashionable private sleuth, aren't you?'

'Not a pretty description – but it suffices,' said Poirot.

The girl sat down on the edge of the kitchen table. She felt in her bag for a cigarette. She placed it between her lips, lighted it, and then said in between two puffs of smoke:

'Somehow, I don't see what M. Hercule Poirot is doing in our humble little crime.'

'Mademoiselle,' said Poirot. 'What you do not see and what I do not see would probably fill a volume.

But all that is of no practical importance. What *is* of practical importance is something that will not be easy to find.'

'What's that?'

'Death, mademoiselle, unfortunately creates a *prejudice*. A prejudice in favour of the deceased. I heard what you said just now to my friend Hastings. "A nice bright girl with no men friends." You said that in mockery of the newspapers. And it is very true – when a young girl is dead, that is the kind of thing that is said. She was bright. She was happy. She was sweet-tempered. She had not a care in the world. She had no undesirable acquaintances. There is a great charity always to the dead. Do you know what I should like this minute? I should like to find someone who knew Elizabeth Barnard *and who does not know she is dead*! Then, perhaps, I should hear what is useful to me – the truth.'

Megan Barnard looked at him for a few minutes in silence whilst she smoked. Then, at last, she spoke. Her words made me jump.

'Betty,' she said, 'was an unmitigated little ass!'

Chapter 11

Megan Barnard

As I said, Megan Barnard's words, and still more the crisp businesslike tone in which they were uttered, made me jump.

Poirot, however, merely bowed his head gravely.

'*A la bonne heure*,' he said. 'You are intelligent, mademoiselle.'

Megan Barnard said, still in the same detached tone:

'I was extremely fond of Betty. But my fondness didn't blind me from seeing exactly the kind of silly little fool she was – and even telling her so upon occasions! Sisters are like that.'

'And did she pay any attention to your advice?'

'Probably not,' said Megan cynically.

'Will you, mademoiselle, be precise.'

The girl hesitated for a minute or two.

Poirot said with a slight smile:

'I will help you. I heard what you said to Hastings.

That your sister was a bright, happy girl with no men friends. It was – *un peu* – the *opposite* that was true, was it not?'

Megan said slowly:

'There wasn't any harm in Betty. I want you to understand that. She'd always go straight. She's not the weekending kind. Nothing of that sort. But she liked being taken out and dancing and – oh, cheap flattery and compliments and all that sort of thing.'

'And she was pretty – yes?'

This question, the third time I had heard it, met this time with a practical response.

Megan slipped off the table, went to her suitcase, snapped it open and extracted something which she handed to Poirot.

In a leather frame was a head and shoulders of a fair-haired, smiling girl. Her hair had evidently recently been permed, it stood out from her head in a mass of rather frizzy curls. The smile was arch and artificial. It was certainly not a face that you could call beautiful, but it had an obvious and cheap prettiness.

Poirot handed it back, saying:

'You and she do not resemble each other, mademoiselle.'

'Oh! I'm the plain one of the family. I've always known that.' She seemed to brush aside the fact as unimportant.

'In what way exactly do you consider your sister was behaving foolishly? Do you mean, perhaps, in relation to Mr Donald Fraser?'

'That's it, exactly. Don's a very quiet sort of person – but he – well, naturally he'd resent certain things – and then –'

'And then what, mademoiselle?'

His eyes were on her very steadily.

It may have been my fancy but it seemed to me that she hesitated a second before answering.

'I was afraid that he might – chuck her altogether. And that would have been a pity. He's a very steady and hard-working man and would have made her a good husband.'

Poirot continued to gaze at her. She did not flush under his glance but returned it with one of her own equally steady and with something else in it – something that reminded me of her first defiant, disdainful manner.

'So it is like that,' he said at last. 'We do not speak the truth any longer.'

She shrugged her shoulders and turned towards the door.

'Well,' she said. 'I've done what I could to help you.'

Poirot's voice arrested her.

'Wait, mademoiselle. I have something to tell you. Come back.'

Rather unwillingly, I thought, she obeyed.

Somewhat to my surprise, Poirot plunged into the whole story of the A B C letters, the murder of Andover, and the railway guide found by the bodies.

He had no reason to complain of any lack of interest on her part. Her lips parted, her eyes gleaming, she hung on his words.

'Is this all true, M. Poirot?'

'Yes, it is true.'

'You really mean that my sister was killed by some horrible homicidal maniac?'

'Precisely?'

She drew a deep breath.

'Oh! Betty – Betty – how – how *ghastly*!'

'You see, mademoiselle, that the information for which I ask you can give freely without wondering whether or not it will hurt anyone.'

'Yes, I see that now.'

'Then let us continue our conversation. I have formed the idea that this Donald Fraser has, perhaps, a violent and jealous temper, is that right?'

Megan Barnard said quietly:

'I'm trusting you now, M. Poirot. I'm going to give you the absolute truth. Don is, as I say, a very quiet person – a bottled-up person, if you know what I mean. He can't always express what he feels in words. But underneath it all he minds things terribly. And he's got a jealous nature. He was always jealous of Betty. He was devoted to her – and of course she was very fond of him, but it wasn't in Betty to be fond of one person and not notice anybody else. She wasn't made that way. She'd got a – well, an eye for any nice-looking man who'd pass the time of day with her. And of course, working in the Ginger Cat, she was always running up against men – especially in the summer holidays. She was always very pat with her tongue and if they chaffed her she'd chaff back again. And then perhaps she'd meet them and go to the pictures or something like that. Nothing serious – never anything of that kind – but she just liked her fun. She used to say that as she'd got to settle down with Don one day she might as well have her fun now while she could.'

Megan paused and Poirot said:

'I understand. Continue.'

'It was just that attitude of mind of hers that Don couldn't understand. If she was really keen on him he couldn't see why she wanted to go out with other people. And once or twice they had flaming big rows about it.'

'M. Don, he was no longer quiet?'

'It's like all those quiet people, when they do lose their tempers they lose them with a vengeance. Don was so violent that Betty was frightened.'

'When was this?'

'There was one row nearly a year ago and another – a worse one – just over a month ago. I was home for the weekend – and I got them to patch it up again, and it was then I tried to knock a little sense into Betty – told her she was a little fool. All she would say was that there hadn't been any harm in it. Well, that was true enough, but all the same she was riding for a fall. You see, after the row a year ago, she'd got into the habit of telling a few useful lies on the principle that what the mind doesn't know the heart doesn't grieve over. This last flare-up came because she'd told Don she was going to Hastings to see a girl pal – and he found out that she'd really been over to Eastbourne with some man. He was a married man, as it happened, and he'd been a bit secretive about the business anyway – and so that made it worse. They had an awful scene – Betty saying that she wasn't married to him yet and she had a right to go about with whom she pleased and Don all white and shaking and saying that one day – one day –'

'Yes?'

'He'd commit murder –' said Megan in a lowered voice.

She stopped and stared at Poirot.

He nodded his head gravely several times.

'And so, naturally, you were afraid . . .'

'I didn't think he'd actually done it – not for a minute! But I was afraid it might be brought up – the quarrel and all that he'd said – several people knew about it.'

Again Poirot nodded his head gravely.

'Just so. And I may say, mademoiselle, that but for the egoistical vanity of a killer, that is just what would have happened. If Donald Fraser escapes suspicion, it will be thanks to A B C's maniacal boasting.'

He was silent for a minute or two, then he said:

'Do you know if your sister met this married man, or any other man, lately?'

Megan shook her head.

'I don't know. I've been away, you see.'

'But what do you think?'

'She mayn't have met that particular man again. He'd probably sheer off if he thought there was a chance of a row, but it wouldn't surprise me if Betty had – well, been telling Don a few lies again. You see, she did so enjoy dancing and the pictures, and of course, Don couldn't afford to take her all the time.'

'If so, is she likely to have confided in anyone? The girl at the café, for instance?'

'I don't think that's likely. Betty couldn't bear the Higley girl. She thought her common. And the others would be new. Betty wasn't the confiding sort anyway.'

An electric bell trilled sharply above the girl's head.

She went to the window and leaned out. She drew back her head sharply.

'It's Don . . .'

'Bring him in here,' said Poirot quickly. 'I would like a word with him before our good inspector takes him in hand.'

Like a flash Megan Barnard was out of the kitchen, and a couple of seconds later she was back again leading Donald Fraser by the hand.

Chapter 12

Donald Fraser

I felt sorry at once for the young man. His white haggard face and bewildered eyes showed how great a shock he had had.

He was a well-made, fine-looking young fellow, standing close on six foot, not good-looking, but with a pleasant, freckled face, high cheek-bones and flaming red hair.

'What's this, Megan?' he said. 'Why in here? For God's sake, tell me – I've only just heard – Betty . . .'

His voice trailed away.

Poirot pushed forward a chair and he sank down on it.

My friend then extracted a small flask from his pocket, poured some of its contents into a convenient cup which was hanging on the dresser and said:

'Drink some of this, Mr Fraser. It will do you good.'

The young man obeyed. The brandy brought a little

colour back into his face. He sat up straighter and turned once more to the girl. His manner was quite quiet and self-controlled.

'It's true, I suppose?' he said. 'Betty is – dead – killed?'

'It's true, Don.'

He said as though mechanically:

'Have you just come down from London?'

'Yes. Dad phoned me.'

'By the 9.30, I suppose?' said Donald Fraser.

His mind, shrinking from reality, ran for safety along these unimportant details.

'Yes.'

There was silence for a minute or two, then Fraser said:

'The police? Are they doing anything?'

'They're upstairs now. Looking through Betty's things, I suppose.'

'They've no idea who –? They don't know –?'

He stopped.

He had all a sensitive, shy person's dislike of putting violent facts into words.

Poirot moved forward a little and asked a question. He spoke in a businesslike, matter-of-fact voice as though what he asked was an unimportant detail.

'Did Miss Barnard tell you where she was going last night?'

Fraser replied to the question. He seemed to be speaking mechanically:

'She told me she was going with a girl friend to St Leonards.'

'Did you believe her?'

'I –' Suddenly the automaton came to life. 'What the devil do you mean?'

His face then, menacing, convulsed by sudden passion, made me understand that a girl might well be afraid of rousing his anger.

Poirot said crisply:

'Betty Barnard was killed by a homicidal murderer. Only by speaking the exact truth can you help us to get on his track.'

His glance for a minute turned to Megan.

'That's right, Don,' she said. 'It isn't a time for considering one's own feelings or anyone else's. You've got to come clean.'

Donald Fraser looked suspiciously at Poirot.

'Who are you? You don't belong to the police?'

'I am better than the police,' said Poirot. He said it without conscious arrogance. It was, to him, a simple statement of fact.

'Tell him,' said Megan.

Donald Fraser capitulated.

'I – wasn't sure,' he said. 'I believed her when she said it. Never thought of doing anything else. Afterwards –

perhaps it was something in her manner. I – I, well, I began to wonder.'

'Yes?' said Poirot.

He had sat down opposite Donald Fraser. His eyes, fixed on the other man's, seemed to be exercising a mesmeric spell.

'I was ashamed of myself for being so suspicious. But – but I *was* suspicious . . . I thought of going to the front and watching her when she left the café. I actually went there. Then I felt I couldn't do that. Betty would see me and she'd be angry. She'd realize at once that I was watching her.'

'What did you do?'

'I went over to St Leonards. Got over there by eight o'clock. Then I watched the buses – to see if she were in them . . . But there was no sign of her . . .'

'And then?'

'I – I lost my head rather. I was convinced she was with some man. I thought it probable he had taken her in his car to Hastings. I went on there – looked in hotels and restaurants, hung round cinemas – went on the pier. All damn foolishness. Even if she was there I was unlikely to find her, and anyway, there were heaps of other places he might have taken her to instead of Hastings.'

He stopped. Precise as his tone had remained, I caught an undertone of that blind, bewildering misery and anger that had possessed him at the time he described.

'In the end I gave it up – came back.'

'At what time?'

'I don't know. I walked. It must have been midnight or after when I got home.'

'Then –'

The kitchen door opened.

'Oh, there you are,' said Inspector Kelsey.

Inspector Crome pushed past him, shot a glance at Poirot and a glance at the two strangers.

'Miss Megan Barnard and Mr Donald Fraser,' said Poirot, introducing them.

'This is Inspector Crome from London,' he explained.

Turning to the inspector, he said:

'While you pursued your investigations upstairs I have been conversing with Miss Barnard and Mr Fraser, endeavouring if I could to find something that will throw light upon the matter.'

'Oh, yes?' said Inspector Crome, his thoughts not upon Poirot but upon the two newcomers.

Poirot retreated to the hall. Inspector Kelsey said kindly as he passed:

'Get anything?'

But his attention was distracted by his colleague and he did not wait for a reply.

I joined Poirot in the hall.

'Did anything strike you, Poirot?' I inquired.

'Only the amazing magnanimity of the murderer, Hastings.'

I had not the courage to say that I had not the least idea what he meant.

Chapter 13

A Conference

Conferences!

Much of my memories of the A B C case seem to be of conferences.

Conferences at Scotland Yard. At Poirot's rooms. Official conferences. Unofficial conferences.

This particular conference was to decide whether or not the facts relative to the anonymous letters should or should not be made public in the press.

The Bexhill murder had attracted much more attention than the Andover one.

It had, of course, far more elements of popularity. To begin with the victim was a young and good-looking girl. Also, it had taken place at a popular seaside resort.

All the details of the crime were reported fully and rehashed daily in thin disguises. The A B C railway guide came in for its share of attention. The favourite theory was that it had been bought locally by the murderer and that it was a valuable clue to his identity. It also seemed to show that he had come to the place by train and was intending to leave for London.

The railway guide had not figured at all in the meagre accounts of the Andover murder, so there seemed at present little likelihood of the two crimes being connected in the public eye.

'We've got to decide upon a policy,' said the Assistant Commissioner. 'The thing is – which way will give us the best results? Shall we give the public the facts – enlist their co-operation – after all, it'll be the co-operation of several million people, looking out for a madman –'

'He won't look like a madman,' interjected Dr Thompson.

'– looking out for sales of A B C's – and so on. Against that I suppose there's the advantage of working in the dark – not letting our man know what we're up to, but then there's the fact that *he knows very well that we know*. He's drawn attention to himself deliberately by his letters. Eh, Crome, what's your opinion?'

'I look at it this way, sir. If you make it public, *you're playing A B C's game*. That's what he wants – publicity – notoriety. That's what he's out after. I'm right, aren't I, doctor? He wants to make a splash.'

Thompson nodded.

The Assistant Commissioner said thoughtfully:

'So you're for balking him. Refusing him the publicity he's hankering after. What about you, M. Poirot?'

Poirot did not speak for a minute. When he did it was with an air of choosing his words carefully.

'It is difficult for me, Sir Lionel,' he said. 'I am, as you might say, an interested party. The challenge was sent to me. If I say "Suppress that fact – do not make it public," may it not be thought that it is my vanity that speaks? That I am afraid for my reputation? It is difficult! To speak out – to tell all – that has its advantages. It is, at least, a warning . . . On the other hand, I am as convinced as Inspector Crome *that it is what the murderer wants us to do*.'

'H'm!' said the Assistant Commissioner, rubbing his chin. He looked across at Dr Thompson. 'Suppose we refuse our lunatic the satisfaction of the publicity he craves. What's he likely to do?'

'Commit another crime,' said the doctor promptly. 'Force your hand.'

'And if we splash the thing about in headlines. Then what's his reaction?'

'Same answer. One way you *feed* his megalomania, the other you *balk* it. The result's the same. Another crime.'

'What do you say, M. Poirot?'

'I agree with Dr Thompson.'

'A cleft stick – eh? How many crimes do you think this – lunatic has in mind?'

Dr Thompson looked across at Poirot.

'Looks like A to Z,' he said cheerfully.

'Of course,' he went on, 'he won't get there. Not nearly. You'll have him by the heels long before that. Interesting to know how he'd have dealt with the letter X.' He recalled himself guiltily from this purely enjoyable speculation. 'But you'll have him long before that. G or H, let's say.'

The Assistant Commissioner struck the table with his fist.

'My God, are you telling me we're going to have five more murders?'

'It won't be as much as that, sir,' said Inspector Crome. 'Trust me.'

He spoke with confidence.

'Which letter of the alphabet do you place it at, inspector?' asked Poirot.

There was a slight ironic note in his voice. Crome, I thought, looked at him with a tinge of dislike adulterating the usual calm superiority.

'Might get him next time, M. Poirot. At any rate, I'd guarantee to get him by the time he gets to F.'

He turned to the Assistant Commissioner.

'I think I've got the psychology of the case fairly clear. Dr Thompson will correct me if I'm wrong. I take it that every time A B C brings a crime off, his self-confidence increases about a hundred per cent. Every time he feels "I'm clever – they can't catch me!" he becomes so over-weeningly confident that he also becomes careless. He exaggerates his own cleverness and everyone else's stupidity. Very soon he'd be hardly bothering to take any precautions at all. That's right, isn't it, doctor?'

Thompson nodded.

'That's usually the case. In non-medical terms it couldn't have been put better. You know something about such things, M. Poirot. Don't you agree?'

I don't think that Crome liked Thompson's appeal to Poirot. He considered that he and he only was the expert on this subject.

'It is as Inspector Crome says,' agreed Poirot.

'Paranoia,' murmured the doctor.

Poirot turned to Crome.

'Are there any material facts of interest in the Bexhill case?'

'Nothing very definite. A waiter at the Splendide at Eastbourne recognizes the dead girl's photograph as that of a young woman who dined there on the evening of the 24th in company with a middle-aged man in spectacles. It's also been recognized at a roadhouse place called the Scarlet Runner halfway between Bexhill and London. They say she was there about 9 pm on the

24th with a man who looked like a naval officer. They can't both be right, but either of them's probable. Of course, there's a host of other identifications, but most of them not good for much. We haven't been able to trace the A B C.'

'Well, you seem to be doing all that can be done, Crome,' said the Assistant Commissioner. 'What do you say, M. Poirot? Does any line of inquiry suggest itself to you?'

Poirot said slowly:

'It seems to me that there is one very important clue – the discovery of the motive.'

'Isn't that pretty obvious? An alphabetical complex. Isn't that what you called it, doctor?'

'*Ça, oui*,' said Poirot. 'There is an alphabetical complex. But why an alphabetical complex? A madman in particular has always a very strong reason for the crimes he commits.'

'Come, come, M. Poirot,' said Crome. 'Look at Stoneman in 1929. He ended by trying to do away with anyone who annoyed him in the slightest degree.'

Poirot turned to him.

'Quite so. But if you are a sufficiently great and important person, it is necessary that you should be spared small annoyances. If a fly settles on your forehead again and again, maddening you by its tickling – what do you do? You endeavour to kill that fly. You have no qualms about it. *You* are important – the fly is not. You kill the fly and the annoyance ceases. Your action appears to you sane and justifiable. Another reason for killing a fly is if you have a strong passion for hygiene. The fly is a potential source of danger to the community – the fly must go. So works the mind of the mentally deranged criminal. But consider now this case – *if the victims are alphabetically selected, then they are not being removed because they are a source of annoyance to the murderer personally*. It would be too much of a coincidence to combine the two.'

'That's a point,' said Dr Thompson. 'I remember a case where a woman's husband was condemned to death. She started killing the members of the jury one by one. Quite a time before the crimes were connected up. They seemed entirely haphazard. But as M. Poirot says, there isn't such a thing as a murderer who commits crimes at *random*. Either he removes people who stand (however insignificantly) in his path, or else he kills by *conviction*. He removes clergymen, or policemen, or prostitutes because he firmly believes that they *should* be removed. That doesn't apply here either as far as I can see. Mrs Ascher and Betty Barnard cannot be linked as members of the same class. Of course, it's possible that there is a sex complex. Both victims have been women. We can tell better, of course, after the next crime –'

'For God's sake, Thompson, don't speak so glibly of the next crime,' said Sir Lionel irritably. 'We're going to do all we can to prevent another crime.'

Dr Thompson held his peace and blew his nose with some violence.

'Have it your own way,' the noise seemed to say. 'If you won't face facts –'

The Assistant Commissioner turned to Poirot.

'I see what you're driving at, but I'm not quite clear yet.'

'I ask myself,' said Poirot, 'what passes exactly in the mind of the murderer? He kills, it would seem from his letters, *pour le sport* – to amuse himself. Can that really be true? And even if it is true, on what principle does he select his victims *apart from the merely alphabetical one*? If he kills merely to amuse himself he would not advertise the fact, since, otherwise, he could kill with impunity. But no, he seeks, as we all agree, to make the splash in the public eye – to assert his personality. In what way has his personality been suppressed that one can connect with the two victims he has so far selected? A final suggestion: Is his motive direct personal hatred of *me*, of Hercule Poirot? Does he challenge me in public because I have (unknown to myself) vanquished him somewhere in the course of my career? Or is his animosity impersonal – directed against a *foreigner*? And if so, what again has led to that? What injury has he suffered at a foreigner's hand?'

'All very suggestive questions,' said Dr Thompson.

Inspector Crome cleared his throat.

'Oh, yes? A little unanswerable at present, perhaps.'

'Nevertheless, my friend,' said Poirot, looking straight at him, '*it is there, in those questions, that the solution lies.* If we knew the exact reason – fantastic, perhaps, to us – but logical to him – of *why* our madman commits these crimes, we should know, perhaps, who the next victim is likely to be.'

Crome shook his head.

'He selects them haphazard – that's my opinion.'

'The magnanimous murderer,' said Poirot.

'What's that you say?'

'I said – the magnanimous murderer! Franz Ascher would have been arrested for the murder of his wife – Donald Fraser might have been arrested for the murder of Betty Barnard – if it had not been for the warning letters of A B C. Is he, then, so soft-hearted that he cannot bear others to suffer for something they did not do?'

'I've known stranger things happen,' said Dr Thompson. 'I've known men who've killed half a dozen victims all broken up because one of their victims didn't die instantaneously and suffered pain. All the same, I don't think that that is our fellow's reason.

He wants the credit of these crimes for his own honour and glory. That's the explanation that fits best.'

'We've come to no decision about the publicity business,' said the Assistant Commissioner.

'If I may make a suggestion, sir,' said Crome. 'Why not wait till the receipt of the next letter? Make it public then – special editions, etc. It will make a bit of a panic in the particular town named, but it will put everyone whose name begins with C on their guard, and it'll put A B C on his mettle. He'll be determined to succeed. And that's when we'll get him.'

How little we knew what the future held.

Chapter 14

The Third Letter

I well remember the arrival of A B C's third letter.

I may say that all precautions had been taken so that when A B C resumed his campaign there should be no unnecessary delays. A young sergeant from Scotland Yard was attached to the house and if Poirot and I were out it was his duty to open anything that came so as to be able to communicate with headquarters without loss of time.

As the days succeeded each other we had all grown more and more on edge. Inspector Crome's aloof and superior manner grew more and more aloof and superior as one by one his more hopeful clues petered out. The vague descriptions of men said to have been seen with Betty Barnard proved useless. Various cars noticed in the vicinity of Bexhill and Cooden were either accounted for or could not be traced. The investigation of purchases of A B C railway guides caused inconvenience and trouble to heaps of innocent people.

As for ourselves, each time the postman's familiar rat-tat sounded on the door, our hearts beat faster with apprehension. At least that was true for me, and I cannot but believe that Poirot experienced the same sensation.

He was, I knew, deeply unhappy over the case. He refused to leave London, preferring to be on the spot in case of emergency. In those hot dog days even his moustaches drooped – neglected for once by their owner.

It was on a Friday that A B C's third letter came. The evening post arrived about ten o'clock.

When we heard the familiar step and the brisk rat-tat, I rose and went along to the box. There were four or five letters, I remember. The last one I looked at was addressed in printed characters.

'Poirot,' I cried . . . My voice died away.

'It has come? Open it, Hastings. Quickly. Every moment may be needed. We must make our plans.'

I tore open the letter (Poirot for once did not reproach me with untidiness) and extracted the printed sheet.

'Read it,' said Poirot.

I read aloud:

Poor Mr Poirot, – Not so good at these little criminal matters as you thought yourself, are you? Rather past your prime, perhaps? Let us see if you can do any better this time. This time it's an easy one. Churston on the 30th. Do try and do something about it! It's a bit dull having it all *my own way, you know!*

Good hunting. Ever yours,

A B C.

'Churston,' I said, jumping to our own copy of an A B C. 'Let's see where it is.'

'Hastings,' Poirot's voice came sharply and interrupted me. 'When was that letter written? Is there a date on it?'

I glanced at the letter in my hand.

'Written on the 27th,' I announced.

'Did I hear you aright, Hastings? Did he give the date of the murder as the *30th*?'

'That's right. Let me see, that's –'

'*Bon Dieu*, Hastings – do you not realise? *Today is the 30th*.'

His eloquent hand pointed to the calendar on the wall. I caught up the daily paper to confirm it.

'But why – how –' I stammered.

Poirot caught up the torn envelope from the floor. Something unusual about the address had registered itself vaguely in my brain, but I had been too anxious to get at the contents of the letter to pay more than fleeting attention to it.

Poirot was at the time living in Whitehaven Mansions. The address ran: *M. Hercule Poirot, Whitehorse Mansions*, across the corner was scrawled: '*Not known at Whitehorse Mansions, EC1, nor at Whitehorse Court – try Whitehaven Mansions.*'

'*Mon Dieu!*' murmured Poirot. 'Does even chance aid this madman? *Vite – vite* – we must get on to Scotland Yard.'

A minute or two later we were speaking to Crome over the wire. For once the self-controlled inspector did not reply 'Oh, yes?' Instead a quickly stifled curse came to his lips. He heard what we had to say, then rang off in order to get a trunk connection to Churston as rapidly as possible.

'*C'est trop tard*,' murmured Poirot.

'You can't be sure of that,' I argued, though without any great hope.

He glanced at the clock.

'Twenty minutes past ten? An hour and forty minutes to go. Is it likely that A B C will have held his hand so long?'

I opened the railway guide I had previously taken from its shelf.

'Churston, Devon,' I read, 'from Paddington 204¾ miles. Population 656. It sounds a fairly small place.

Surely our man will be bound to be noticed there.'

'Even so, another life will have been taken,' murmured Poirot. 'What are the trains? I imagine train will be quicker than car.'

'There's a midnight train – sleeping car to Newton Abbot – gets there 6.8 am, and then Churston at 7.15.'

'That is from Paddington?'

'Paddington, yes.'

'We will take that, Hastings.'

'You'll hardly have time to get news before we start.'

'If we receive bad news tonight or tomorrow morning does it matter which?'

'There's something in that.'

I put a few things together in a suitcase while Poirot once more rang up Scotland Yard.

A few minutes later he came into the bedroom and demanded:

'*Mais qu'est ce que vous faites là?*'

'I was packing for you. I thought it would save time.'

'*Vous éprouvez trop d'émotion, Hastings*. It affects your hands and your wits. Is that a way to fold a coat? And regard what you have done to my pyjamas. If the hairwash breaks what will befall them?'

'Good heavens, Poirot,' I cried, 'this is a matter of life and death. What does it matter what happens to our clothes?'

'You have no sense of proportion, Hastings. We cannot catch a train earlier than the time that it leaves, and to ruin one's clothes will not be the least helpful in preventing a murder.'

Taking his suitcase from me firmly, he took the packing into his own hands.

He explained that we were to take the letter and envelope to Paddington with us. Someone from Scotland Yard would meet us there.

When we arrived on the platform the first person we saw was Inspector Crome.

He answered Poirot's look of inquiry.

'No news as yet. All men available are on the lookout. All persons whose name begins with C are being warned by phone when possible. There's just a chance. Where's the letter?'

Poirot gave it to him.

He examined it, swearing softly under his breath.

'Of all the damned luck. The stars in their courses fight for the fellow.'

'You don't think,' I suggested, 'that it was done on purpose?'

Crome shook his head.

'No. He's got his rules – crazy rules – and abides by them. Fair warning. He makes a point of that. That's where his boastfulness comes in. I wonder now – I'd almost bet the chap drinks White Horse whisky.'

'*Ah, c'est ingénieux, ça!*' said Poirot, driven to admiration in spite of himself. 'He prints the letter and the bottle is in front of him.'

'That's the way of it,' said Crome. 'We've all of us done much the same thing one time or another, unconsciously copied something that's just under the eye. He started off White and went on horse instead of haven . . .'

The inspector, we found, was also travelling by the train.

'Even if by some unbelievable luck nothing happened, Churston is the place to be. Our murderer is there, or has been there today. One of my men is on the phone here up to the last minute in case anything comes through.'

Just as the train was leaving the station we saw a man running down the platform. He reached the inspector's window and called up something.

As the train drew out of the station Poirot and I hurried along the corridor and tapped on the door of the inspector's sleeper.

'You have news – yes?' demanded Poirot.

Crome said quietly:

'It's about as bad as it can be. Sir Carmichael Clarke has been found with his head bashed in.'

Sir Carmichael Clarke, although his name was not very well known to the general public, was a man of some eminence. He had been in his time a very well-known throat specialist. Retiring from his profession very comfortably off, he had been able to indulge what had been one of the chief passions of his life – a collection of Chinese pottery and porcelain. A few years later, inheriting a considerable fortune from an elderly uncle, he had been able to indulge his passion to the full, and he was now the possessor of one of the best-known collections of Chinese art. He was married but had no children and lived in a house he had built for himself near the Devon coast, only coming to London on rare occasions such as when some important sale was on.

It did not require much reflection to realize that his death, following that of the young and pretty Betty Barnard, would provide the best newspaper sensation for years. The fact that it was August and that the papers were hard up for subject matter would make matters worse.

'*Eh bien*,' said Poirot. 'It is possible that publicity may do what private efforts have failed to do. The whole country now will be looking for A B C.'

'Unfortunately,' I said, 'that's what he wants.'

'True. But it may, all the same, be his undoing. Gratified by success, he may become careless . . . That is what I hope – that he may be drunk with his own cleverness.'

'How odd all this is, Poirot,' I exclaimed, struck suddenly by an idea. 'Do you know, this is the first crime of this kind that you and I have worked on together? All our murders have been – well, private murders, so to speak.'

'You are quite right, my friend. Always, up to now, it has fallen to our lot to work from the *inside*. It has been the history of the *victim* that was important. The important points have been: "Who benefited by the death? What opportunities had those round him to commit the crime?" It has always been the "*crime intime*". Here, for the first time in our association, it is cold-blooded, impersonal murder. Murder from the *outside*.'

I shivered.

'It's rather horrible . . .'

'Yes. I felt from the first, when I read the original letter, that there was something wrong – misshapen . . .'

He made an impatient gesture.

'One must not give way to the nerves . . . *This is no worse than any ordinary crime* . . .'

'It is . . . It is . . .'

'Is it worse to take the life or lives of strangers than to take the life of someone near and dear to you – someone who trusts and believes in you, perhaps?'

'It's worse because it's *mad* . . .'

'No, Hastings. It is not *worse.* It is only more *difficult.*'

'No, no, I do not agree with you. It's infinitely more frightening.'

Hercule Poirot said thoughtfully:

'It should be easier to discover because it is mad. A crime committed by someone shrewd and sane would be far more complicated. Here, if one could but hit on the *idea* . . . This alphabetical business, it has discrepancies. If I could once see the *idea* – then everything would be clear and simple . . .'

He sighed and shook his head.

'These crimes must not go on. Soon, soon, I must see the truth . . . Go, Hastings. Get some sleep. There will be much to do tomorrow.'

Chapter 15

Sir Carmichael Clarke

Churston, lying as it does between Brixham on the one side and Paignton and Torquay on the other, occupies a position about half-way round the curve of Torbay. Until about ten years ago it was merely a golf links and below the links a green sweep of countryside dropping down to the sea with only a farmhouse or two in the way of human occupation. But of late years there had been big building developments between Churston and Paignton and the coastline is now dotted with small houses and bungalows, new roads, etc.

Sir Carmichael Clarke had purchased a site of some two acres commanding an uninterrupted view of the sea. The house he had built was of modern design – a white rectangle that was not unpleasing to the eye. Apart from two big galleries that housed his collection it was not a large house.

Our arrival there took place about 8 am. A local

police officer had met us at the station and had put us *au courant* of the situation.

Sir Carmichael Clarke, it seemed, had been in the habit of taking a stroll after dinner every evening. When the police rang up – at some time after eleven – it was ascertained that he had not returned. Since his stroll usually followed the same course, it was not long before a search-party discovered his body. Death was due to a crashing blow with some heavy instrument on the back of the head. *An open A B C had been placed face downwards on the dead body.*

We arrived at Combeside (as the house was called) at about eight o'clock. The door was opened by an elderly butler whose shaking hands and disturbed face showed how much the tragedy had affected him.

'Good morning, Deveril,' said the police officer.

'Good morning, Mr Wells.'

'These are the gentlemen from London, Deveril.'

'This way, gentlemen.' He ushered us into a long dining-room where breakfast was laid. 'I'll get Mr Franklin.'

A minute or two later a big fair-haired man with a sunburnt face entered the room.

This was Franklin Clarke, the dead man's only brother.

He had the resolute competent manner of a man accustomed to meeting with emergencies.

'Good morning, gentlemen.'

Inspector Wells made the introductions.

'This is Inspector Crome of the CID, Mr Hercule Poirot and – er – Captain Hayter.'

'Hastings,' I corrected coldly.

Franklin Clarke shook hands with each of us in turn and in each case the handshake was accompanied by a piercing look.

'Let me offer you some breakfast,' he said. 'We can discuss the position as we eat.'

There were no dissentient voices and we were soon doing justice to excellent eggs and bacon and coffee.

'Now for it,' said Franklin Clarke. 'Inspector Wells gave me a rough idea of the position last night – though I may say it seemed one of the wildest tales I have ever heard. Am I really to believe, Inspector Crome, that my poor brother is the victim of a homicidal maniac, that this is the third murder that has occurred and that *in each case an A B C railway guide has been deposited beside the body*?'

'That is substantially the position, Mr Clarke.'

'But *why*? What earthly benefit can accrue from such a crime – even in the most diseased imagination?'

Poirot nodded his head in approval.

'You go straight to the point, Mr Franklin,' he said.

'It's not much good looking for motives at this stage, Mr Clarke,' said Inspector Crome. 'That's a matter for an alienist – though I may say that I've had a certain experience of criminal lunacy and that the motives are usually grossly inadequate. There is a desire to assert one's personality, to make a splash in the public eye – in fact, to be a somebody instead of a nonentity.'

'Is that true, M. Poirot?'

Clarke seemed incredulous. His appeal to the older man was not too well received by Inspector Crome, who frowned.

'Absolutely true,' replied my friend.

'At any rate such a man cannot escape detection long,' said Clarke thoughtfully.

'*Vous croyez?* Ah, but they are cunning – *ces gens là!* And you must remember *such a type has usually all the outer signs of insignificance* – he belongs to the class of person who is usually passed over and ignored or even laughed at!'

'Will you let me have a few facts, please, Mr Clarke,' said Crome, breaking in on the conversation.

'Certainly.'

'Your brother, I take it, was in his usual health and spirits yesterday? He received no unexpected letters? Nothing to upset him?'

'No. I should say he was quite his usual self.'

'Not upset and worried in any way.'

'Excuse me, inspector. I didn't say that. To be upset and worried was my poor brother's normal condition.'

'Why was that?'

'You may not know that my sister-in-law, Lady Clarke, is in very bad health. Frankly, between ourselves, she is suffering from an incurable cancer, and cannot live very much longer. Her illness has preyed terribly on my brother's mind. I myself returned from the East not long ago and I was shocked at the change in him.'

Poirot interpolated a question.

'Supposing, Mr Clarke, that your brother had been found shot at the foot of a cliff – or shot with a revolver beside him. What would have been your first thought?'

'Quite frankly, I should have jumped to the conclusion that it was suicide,' said Clarke.

'*Encore!*' said Poirot.

'What is that?'

'A fact that repeats itself. It is of no matter.'

'Anyway, it *wasn't* suicide,' said Crome with a touch of curtness. 'Now I believe, Mr Clarke, that it was your brother's habit to go for a stroll every evening?'

'Quite right. He always did.'

'Every night?'

'Well, not if it was pouring with rain, naturally.'

'And everyone in the house knew of this habit?'

'Of course.'

'And outside?'

'I don't quite know what you mean by outside.

The gardener may have been aware of it or not, I don't know.'

'And in the village?'

'Strictly speaking, we haven't got a village. There's a post office and cottages at Churston Ferrers – but there's no village or shops.'

'I suppose a stranger hanging round the place would be fairly easily noticed?'

'On the contrary. In August all this part of the world is a seething mass of strangers. They come over every day from Brixham and Torquay and Paignton in cars and buses and on foot. Broadsands, which is down there (he pointed), is a very popular beach and so is Elbury Cove – it's a well-known beauty spot and people come there and picnic. I wish they didn't! You've no idea how beautiful and peaceful this part of the world is in June and the beginning of July.'

'So you don't think a stranger would be noticed?'

'Not unless he looked – well, off his head.'

'This man doesn't look off his head,' said Crome with certainty. 'You see what I'm getting at, Mr Clarke. This man must have been spying out the land beforehand and discovered your brother's habit of taking an evening stroll. I suppose, by the way, that no strange man came up to the house and asked to see Sir Carmichael yesterday?'

'Not that I know of – but we'll ask Deveril.'

He rang the bell and put the question to the butler.

'No, sir, no one came to see Sir Carmichael. And I didn't notice anyone hanging about the house either. No more did the maids, because I've asked them.'

The butler waited a moment, then inquired: 'Is that all, sir?'

'Yes, Deveril, you can go.'

The butler withdrew, drawing back in the doorway to let a young woman pass.

Franklin Clarke rose as she came in.

'This is Miss Grey, gentlemen. My brother's secretary.'

My attention was caught at once by the girl's extraordinary Scandinavian fairness. She had the almost colourless ash hair – light-grey eyes – and transparent glowing pallor that one finds amongst Norwegians and Swedes. She looked about twenty-seven and seemed to be as efficient as she was decorative.

'Can I help you in any way?' she asked as she sat down.

Clarke brought her a cup of coffee, but she refused any food.

'Did you deal with Sir Carmichael's correspondence?' asked Crome.

'Yes, all of it.'

'I suppose he never received a letter or letters signed A B C?'

'A B C?' She shook her head. 'No, I'm sure he didn't.'

'He didn't mention having seen anyone hanging about during his evening walks lately?'

'No. He never mentioned anything of the kind.'

'And you yourself have noticed no strangers?'

'Not exactly hanging about. Of course, there are a lot of people what you might call *wandering* about at this time of year. One often meets people strolling with an aimless look across the golf links or down the lanes to the sea. In the same way, practically everyone one sees this time of year is a stranger.'

Poirot nodded thoughtfully.

Inspector Crome asked to be taken over the ground of Sir Carmichael's nightly walk. Franklin Clarke led the way through the french window, and Miss Grey accompanied us.

She and I were a little behind the others.

'All this must have been a terrible shock to you all,' I said.

'It seems quite unbelievable. I had gone to bed last night when the police rang up. I heard voices downstairs and at last I came out and asked what was the matter. Deveril and Mr Clarke were just setting out with lanterns.'

'What time did Sir Carmichael usually come back from his walk?'

'About a quarter to ten. He used to let himself in by the side door and then sometimes he went straight to bed, sometimes to the gallery where his collections were. That is why, unless the police had rung up, he would probably not have been missed till they went to call him this morning.'

'It must have been a terrible shock to his wife?'

'Lady Clarke is kept under morphia a good deal. I think she is in too dazed a condition to appreciate what goes on round her.'

We had come out through a garden gate on to the golf links. Crossing a corner of them, we passed over a stile into a steep, winding lane.

'This leads down to Elbury Cove,' explained Franklin Clarke. 'But two years ago they made a new road leading from the main road to Broadsands and on to Elbury, so that now this lane is practically deserted.'

We went on down the lane. At the foot of it a path led between brambles and bracken down to the sea. Suddenly we came out on a grassy ridge overlooking the sea and a beach of glistening white stones. All round dark green trees ran down to the sea. It was an enchanting spot – white, deep green – and sapphire blue.

'How beautiful!' I exclaimed.

Clarke turned to me eagerly.

'Isn't it? Why people want to go abroad to the Riviera

when they've got this! I've wandered all over the world in my time and, honest to God, I've never seen anything as beautiful.'

Then, as though ashamed of his eagerness, he said in a more matter-of-fact tone:

'This was my brother's evening walk. He came as far as here, then back up the path, and turning to the right instead of the left, went past the farm and across the fields back to the house.'

We proceeded on our way till we came to a spot near the hedge, half-way across the field where the body had been found.

Crome nodded.

'Easy enough. The man stood here in the shadow. Your brother would have noticed nothing till the blow fell.'

The girl at my side gave a quick shiver.

Franklin Clarke said:

'Hold up, Thora. It's pretty beastly, but it's no use shirking facts.'

Thora Grey – the name suited her.

We went back to the house where the body had been taken after being photographed.

As we mounted the wide staircase the doctor came out of a room, black bag in hand.

'Anything to tell us, doctor?' inquired Clarke.

The doctor shook his head.

'Perfectly simple case. I'll keep the technicalities for the inquest. Anyway, he didn't suffer. Death must have been instantaneous.'

He moved away.

'I'll just go in and see Lady Clarke.'

A hospital nurse came out of a room farther along the corridor and the doctor joined her.

We went into the room out of which the doctor had come.

I came out again rather quickly. Thora Grey was still standing at the head of the stairs.

There was a queer scared expression on her face.

'Miss Grey –' I stopped. 'Is anything the matter?'

She looked at me.

'I was thinking,' she said, 'about D.'

'About D?' I stared at her stupidly.

'Yes. The next murder. Something must be done. It's got to be stopped.'

Clarke came out of the room behind me.

He said:

'What's got to be stopped, Thora?'

'These awful murders.'

'Yes.' His jaw thrust itself out aggressively. 'I want to talk to M. Poirot some time . . . Is Crome any good?' He shot the words out unexpectedly.

I replied that he was supposed to be a very clever officer.

My voice was perhaps not as enthusiastic as it might have been.

'He's got a damned offensive manner,' said Clarke. 'Looks as though he knows everything – and what *does* he know? Nothing at all as far as I can make out.'

He was silent for a minute or two. Then he said:

'M. Poirot's the man for my money. I've got a plan. But we'll talk of that later.'

He went along the passage and tapped at the same door as the doctor had entered.

I hesitated a moment. The girl was staring in front of her.

'What are you thinking of, Miss Grey?'

She turned her eyes towards me.

'I'm wondering *where he is now* . . . the murderer, I mean. It's not twelve hours yet since it happened . . . Oh! aren't there any *real* clairvoyants who could see where he is now and what he is doing . . .'

'The police are searching –' I began.

My commonplace words broke the spell. Thora Grey pulled herself together.

'Yes,' she said. 'Of course.'

In her turn she descended the staircase. I stood there a moment longer conning her words over in my mind.

A B C . . .

Where was he now . . . ?

Chapter 16

Not from Captain Hastings' Personal Narrative

Mr Alexander Bonaparte Cust came out with the rest of the audience from the Torquay Palladium, where he had been seeing and hearing that highly emotional film, *Not a Sparrow* . . .

He blinked a little as he came out into the afternoon sunshine and peered round him in that lost-dog fashion that was characteristic of him.

He murmured to himself: 'It's an idea . . .'

Newsboys passed along crying out:

'Latest . . . Homicidal Maniac at Churston . . .'

They carried placards on which was written:

CHURSTON MURDER. LATEST.

Mr Cust fumbled in his pocket, found a coin, and bought a paper. He did not open it at once.

Entering the Princess Gardens, he slowly made his

way to a shelter facing Torquay harbour. He sat down and opened the paper.

There were big headlines:

SIR CARMICHAEL CLARKE MURDERED.

TERRIBLE TRAGEDY AT CHURSTON.

WORK OF A HOMICIDAL MANIAC.

And below them:

> Only a month ago England was shocked and startled by the murder of a young girl, Elizabeth Barnard, at Bexhill. It may be remembered that an A B C railway guide figured in the case. An A B C was also found by the dead body of Sir Carmichael Clarke, and the police incline to the belief that both crimes were committed by the same person. Can it be possible that a homicidal murderer is going the round of our seaside resorts? . . .

A young man in flannel trousers and a bright blue Aertex shirt who was sitting beside Mr Cust remarked:

'Nasty business – eh?'

Mr Cust jumped.

'Oh, very – very –'

His hands, the young man noticed, were trembling so that he could hardly hold the paper.

'You never know with lunatics,' said the young man chattily. 'They don't always look barmy, you know.

Often they seem just the same as you or me . . .'

'I suppose they do,' said Mr Cust.

'It's a fact. Sometimes it's the war what unhinged them – never been right since.'

'I – I expect you're right.'

'I don't hold with wars,' said the young man.

His companion turned on him.

'I don't hold with plague and sleeping sickness and famine and cancer . . . but they happen all the same!'

'War's preventable,' said the young man with assurance.

Mr Cust laughed. He laughed for some time.

The young man was slightly alarmed.

'He's a bit batty himself,' he thought.

Aloud he said:

'Sorry, sir, I expect you were in the war.'

'I was,' said Mr Cust. 'It – it – unsettled me. My head's never been right since. It aches, you know. Aches terribly.'

'Oh! I'm sorry about that,' said the young man awkwardly.

'Sometimes I hardly know what I'm doing . . .'

'Really? Well, I must be getting along,' said the young man and removed himself hurriedly. He knew what people were once they began to talk about their health.

Mr Cust remained with his paper.

He read and reread . . .

People passed to and fro in front of him.

Most of them were talking of the murder . . .

'Awful . . . do you think it was anything to do with the Chinese? Wasn't the waitress in a Chinese café . . .'

'Actually on the golf links . . .'

'I heard it was on the beach . . .'

'– but, darling, we took our tea to Elbury only *yesterday* . . .'

'– police are sure to get him . . .'

'– say he may be arrested any minute now . . .'

'– quite likely he's in Torquay . . . that other woman was who murdered the what do you call 'ems . . .'

Mr Cust folded up the paper very neatly and laid it on the seat. Then he rose and walked sedately along towards the town.

Girls passed him, girls in white and pink and blue, in summery frocks and pyjamas and shorts. They laughed and giggled. Their eyes appraised the men they passed.

Not once did their eyes linger for a second on Mr Cust . . .

He sat down at a little table and ordered tea and Devonshire cream . . .

Chapter 17

Marking Time

With the murder of Sir Carmichael Clarke the A B C mystery leaped into the fullest prominence.

The newspapers were full of nothing else. All sorts of 'clues' were reported to have been discovered. Arrests were announced to be imminent. There were photographs of every person or place remotely connected with the murder. There were interviews with anyone who would give interviews. There were questions asked in Parliament.

The Andover murder was now bracketed with the other two.

It was the belief of Scotland Yard that the fullest publicity was the best chance of laying the murderer by the heels. The population of Great Britain turned itself into an army of amateur sleuths.

The *Daily Flicker* had the grand inspiration of using the caption:

HE MAY BE IN *YOUR* TOWN!

Poirot, of course, was in the thick of things. The letters sent to him were published and facsimiled. He was abused wholesale for not having prevented the crimes and defended on the ground that he was on the point of naming the murderer.

Reporters incessantly badgered him for interviews.

What M. Poirot Says Today.

Which was usually followed by a half-column of imbecilities.

M. Poirot Takes Grave View of Situation.

M. Poirot on the Eve of Success.

Captain Hastings, the great friend of M. Poirot, told our Special Representative . . .

'Poirot,' I would cry. 'Pray believe me. I never said anything of the kind.'

My friend would reply kindly:

'I know, Hastings – I know. The spoken word and the written – there is an astonishing gulf between them. There is a way of turning sentences that completely reverses the original meaning.'

'I wouldn't like you to think I'd said –'

'But do not worry yourself. All this is of no importance. These imbecilities, even, may help.'

'How?'

'*Eh bien*,' said Poirot grimly. 'If our madman reads what I am supposed to have said to the *Daily Blague* today, he will lose all respect for me as an opponent!'

I am, perhaps, giving the impression that nothing practical was being done in the way of investigations. On the contrary, Scotland Yard and the local police of the various counties were indefatigable in following up the smallest clues.

Hotels, people who kept lodgings, boarding-houses – all those within a wide radius of the crimes were questioned minutely.

Hundreds of stories from imaginative people who had 'seen a man looking very queer and rolling his eyes', or 'noticed a man with a sinister face slinking along', were sifted to the last detail. No information, even of the vaguest character, was neglected. Trains, buses, trams, railway porters, conductors, bookstalls, stationers – there was an indefatigable round of questions and verifications.

At least a score of people were detained and questioned until they could satisfy the police as to their movements on the night in question.

The net result was not entirely a blank. Certain statements were borne in mind and noted down as of possible value, but without further evidence they led nowhere.

If Crome and his colleagues were indefatigable,

Poirot seemed to me strangely supine. We argued now and again.

'But what is it that you would have me do, my friend? The routine inquiries, the police make them better than I do. Always – always you want me to run about like the dog.'

'Instead of which you sit at home like – like –'

'A sensible man! My force, Hastings, is in my *brain*, not in my *feet*! All the time, whilst I seem to you idle, I am reflecting.'

'Reflecting?' I cried. 'Is this a time for reflection?'

'Yes, a thousand times yes.'

'But what can you possibly gain by reflection? You know the facts of the three cases by heart.'

'It is not the facts I reflect upon – but the mind of the murderer.'

'The mind of a madman!'

'Precisely. And therefore not to be arrived at in a minute. *When I know what the murderer is like, I shall be able to find out who he is*. And all the time I learn more. After the Andover crime, what did we know about the murderer? Next to nothing at all. After the Bexhill crime? A little more. After the Churston murder? More still. I begin to see – not what *you* would like to see – the outlines of *a face and form* but the outlines of a *mind*. A mind that moves and works in certain definite directions. After the next crime –'

'Poirot!'

My friend looked at me dispassionately.

'But, yes, Hastings, I think it is almost certain there will be another. A lot depends on *la chance*. So far our *inconnu* has been lucky. This time the luck may turn against him. But in any case, after another crime, we shall know infinitely more. Crime is terribly revealing. Try and vary your methods as you will, your tastes, your habits, your attitude of mind, and your soul is revealed by your actions. There are confusing indications – sometimes it is as though there were two intelligences at work – but soon the outline will clear itself, *I shall know*.'

'Who it is?'

'No, Hastings, I shall not know his name and address! I shall know *what kind of a man he is . . .*'

'And then? . . .'

'*Et alors, je vais à la pêche.*'

As I looked rather bewildered, he went on:

'You comprehend, Hastings, an expert fisherman knows exactly what flies to offer to what fish. I shall offer the right kind of fly.'

'And then?'

'And then? And then? You are as bad as the superior Crome with his eternal "Oh, yes?" *Eh bien*, and then he will take the bait and the hook and we will reel in the line . . .'

'In the meantime people are dying right and left.'

'Three people. And there are, what is it – about 120 – road deaths every week?'

'That is entirely different.'

'It is probably exactly the same to those who die. For the others, the relations, the friends – yes, there is a difference, but one thing at least rejoices me in this case.'

'By all means let us hear anything in the nature of rejoicing.'

'*Inutile* to be so sarcastic. It rejoices me that there is here no shadow of guilt to distress the innocent.'

'Isn't this worse?'

'No, no, a thousand times no! There is nothing so terrible as to live in an atmosphere of suspicion – to see eyes watching you and the love in them changing to fear – nothing so terrible as to suspect those near and dear to you – It is poisonous – a miasma. No, the poisoning of life for the innocent, that, at least, we cannot lay at A B C's door.'

'You'll soon be making excuses for the man!' I said bitterly.

'Why not? He may believe himself fully justified. We may, perhaps, end by having sympathy with his point of view.'

'Really, Poirot!'

'Alas! I have shocked you. First my inertia – and then my views.'

I shook my head without replying.

'All the same,' said Poirot after a minute or two. 'I have one project that will please you – since it is active and not passive. Also, it will entail a lot of conversation and practically no thought.'

I did not quite like his tone.

'What is it?' I asked cautiously.

'The extraction from the friends, relations and servants of the victims of all they know.'

'Do you suspect them of keeping things back, then?'

'Not intentionally. But telling everything you know always implies *selection*. If I were to say to you, recount me your day yesterday, you would perhaps reply: "I rose at nine, I breakfasted at half-past, I had eggs and bacon and coffee, I went to my club, etc." You would not include: "I tore my nail and had to cut it. I rang for shaving water. I spilt a little coffee on the tablecloth. I brushed my hat and put it on." One cannot tell *everything*. Therefore one *selects*. At the time of a murder people select what *they* think is important. But quite frequently they think wrong!'

'And how is one to get at the right things?'

'Simply, as I said just now, by conversation. By talking! By discussing a certain happening, or a certain person, or a certain day, over and over again, extra details are bound to arise.'

'What kind of details?'

'Naturally that I do not know or I should not want to find out. But enough time has passed now for ordinary things to reassume their value. It is against all mathematical laws that in three cases of murder there is no single fact nor sentence with a bearing on the case. Some trivial happening, some trivial remark there *must* be which would be a pointer! It is looking for the needle in the haystack, I grant – *but in the haystack there is a needle* – of that I am convinced!'

It seemed to me extremely vague and hazy.

'You do not see it? Your wits are not so sharp as those of a mere servant girl.'

He tossed me over a letter. It was neatly written in a sloping board-school hand.

> *'Dear Sir, – I hope you will forgive the liberty I take in writing to you. I have been thinking a lot since these awful two murders like poor auntie's. It seems as though we're all in the same boat, as it were. I saw the young lady's picture in the paper, the young lady, I mean, that is the sister of the young lady that was killed at Bexhill. I made so bold as to write to her and tell her I was coming to London to get a place and asked if I could come to her or her mother as I said two heads might be better than one and I would not want much wages, but only to find out who this awful fiend is and perhaps we might get at it better if we could say what we knew something might come of it.*

'The young lady wrote very nicely and said as how she worked in an office and lived in a hostel, but she suggested I might write to you and she said she'd been thinking something of the same kind as I had. And she said we were in the same trouble and we ought to stand together. So I am writing, sir, to say I am coming to London and this is my address.

'Hoping I am not troubling you, Yours respectfully,

'Mary Drower.'

'Mary Drower,' said Poirot, 'is a very intelligent girl.'

He picked up another letter.

'Read this.'

It was a line from Franklin Clarke, saying that he was coming to London and would call upon Poirot the following day if not inconvenient.

'Do not despair, *mon ami*,' said Poirot. 'Action is about to begin.'

Chapter 18

Poirot Makes a Speech

Franklin Clarke arrived at three o'clock on the following afternoon and came straight to the point without beating about the bush.

'M. Poirot,' he said, 'I'm not satisfied.'

'No, Mr Clarke?'

'I've no doubt that Crome is a very efficient officer, but, frankly, he puts my back up. That air of his of knowing best! I hinted something of what I had in mind to your friend here when he was down at Churston, but I've had all my brother's affairs to settle up and I haven't been free until now. My idea is, M. Poirot, that we oughtn't to let the grass grow under our feet –'

'Just what Hastings is always saying!'

'– but go right ahead. We've got to get ready for the next crime.'

'So you think there will be a next crime?'

'Don't you?'

'Certainly.'

'Very well, then. I want to get organized.'

'Tell me your idea exactly?'

'I propose, M. Poirot, a kind of special legion – to work under your orders – composed of the friends and relatives of the murdered people.'

'*Une bonne idée.*'

'I'm glad you approve. By putting our heads together I feel we might get at something. Also, when the next warning comes, by being on the spot, one of us might – I don't say it's probable – but we might recognize some person as having been near the scene of a previous crime.'

'I see your idea, and I approve, but you must remember, Mr Clarke, the relations and friends of the other victims are hardly in your sphere of life. They are employed persons and though they might be given a short vacation –'

Franklin Clarke interrupted.

'That's just it. I'm the only person in a position to foot the bill. Not that I'm particularly well off myself, but my brother died a rich man and it will eventually come to me. I propose, as I say, to enrol a special legion, the members to be paid for their services at the same rate as they get habitually, with, of course, the additional expenses.'

'Who do you propose should form this legion?'

'I've been into that. As a matter of fact, I wrote to Miss Megan Barnard – indeed, this is partly her idea. I suggest myself, Miss Barnard, Mr Donald Fraser, who was engaged to the dead girl. Then there is a niece of the Andover woman – Miss Barnard knows her address. I don't think the husband would be of any use to us – I hear he's usually drunk. I also think the Barnards – the father and mother – are a bit old for active campaigning.'

'Nobody else?'

'Well – er – Miss Grey.'

He flushed slightly as he spoke the name.

'Oh! Miss Grey?'

Nobody in the world could put a gentle nuance of irony into a couple of words better than Poirot. About thirty-five years fell away from Franklin Clarke. He looked suddenly like a shy schoolboy.

'Yes. You see, Miss Grey was with my brother for over two years. She knows the countryside and the people round, and everything. I've been away for a year and a half.'

Poirot took pity on him and turned the conversation.

'You have been in the East? In China?'

'Yes. I had a kind of roving commission to purchase things for my brother.'

'Very interesting it must have been. *Eh bien*, Mr

Clarke, I approve very highly of your idea. I was saying to Hastings only yesterday that a *rapprochement* of the people concerned was needed. It is necessary to pool reminiscences, to compare notes – *enfin* to talk the thing over – to talk – to talk – and again to talk. Out of some innocent phrase may come enlightenment.'

A few days later the 'Special Legion' met at Poirot's rooms.

As they sat round looking obediently towards Poirot, who had his place, like the chairman at a board meeting, at the head of the table, I myself passed them, as it were, in review, confirming or revising my first impressions of them.

The three girls were all of them striking-looking – the extraordinary fair beauty of Thora Grey, the dark intensity of Megan Barnard, with her strange Red Indian immobility of face – Mary Drower, neatly dressed in a black coat and skirt, with her pretty, intelligent face. Of the two men, Franklin Clarke, big, bronzed and talkative, Donald Fraser, self-contained and quiet, made an interesting contrast to each other.

Poirot, unable, of course, to resist the occasion, made a little speech.

'Mesdames and Messieurs, you know what we are here for. The police are doing their utmost to track down the criminal. I, too, in my different way. But it seems to me a reunion of those who have a personal interest in the matter – and also, I may say, a personal knowledge of the victims – might have results that an outside investigation cannot pretend to attain.

'Here we have three murders – an old woman, a young girl, an elderly man. Only one thing links these three people together – *the fact that the same person killed them*. That means that *the same person was present in three different localities* and was seen necessarily by a large number of people. That he is a madman in an advanced stage of mania goes without saying. That his appearance and behaviour give no suggestion of such a fact is equally certain. This person – and though I say *he*, remember it may be a man or a woman – has all the devilish cunning of insanity. He has succeeded so far in covering his traces completely. The police have certain vague indications but nothing upon which they can act.

'Nevertheless, there must exist indications which are not vague but certain. To take one particular point – this assassin, he did not arrive at Bexhill at midnight and find conveniently on the beach a young lady whose name began with B –'

'Must we go into that?'

It was Donald Fraser who spoke – the words wrung from him, it seemed, by some inner anguish.

'It is necessary to go into everything, monsieur,' said Poirot, turning to him. 'You are here, not to save your feelings by refusing to think of details, but if necessary to harrow them by going into the matter *au fond*. As I say, it was not *chance* that provided A B C with a victim in Betty Barnard. There must have been deliberate selection on his part – and therefore premeditation. That is to say, he must have reconnoitred the ground *beforehand*. There were facts of which he had informed himself – the best hour for the committing of the crime at Andover – the *mise en scène* at Bexhill – the habits of Sir Carmichael Clarke at Churston. Me, for one, I refuse to believe that there is *no* indication – no slightest hint – that might help to establish his identity.

'I make the assumption that one – or possibly *all* of you – *knows something that they do not know they know*.

'Sooner or later, by reason of your association with one another, something will come to light, will take on a significance as yet undreamed of. It is like the jig-saw puzzle – each of you may have *a piece apparently without meaning, but which when reunited may show a definite portion of the picture as a whole*.'

'Words!' said Megan Barnard.

'Eh?' Poirot looked at her inquiringly.

'What you've been saying. It's just words. It doesn't mean anything.'

She spoke with that kind of desperate intensity that I had come to associate with her personality.

'Words, mademoiselle, are only the outer clothing of ideas.'

'Well, I think it's sense,' said Mary Drower. 'I do really, miss. It's often when you're talking over things that you seem to see your way clear. Your mind gets made up for you sometimes without your knowing how it's happened. Talking leads to a lot of things one way and another.'

'If "least said is soonest mended", it's the converse we want here,' said Franklin Clarke.

'What do you say, Mr Fraser?'

'I rather doubt the practical applicability of what you say, M. Poirot.'

'What do you think, Thora?' asked Clarke.

'I think the principle of talking things over is always sound.'

'Suppose,' suggested Poirot, 'that you all go over your own remembrances of the time preceding the murder. Perhaps you'll start, Mr Clarke.'

'Let me see, on the morning of the day Car was killed I went off sailing. Caught eight mackerel. Lovely out there on the bay. Lunch at home. Irish stew, I remember. Slept in the hammock. Tea. Wrote some letters, missed the post, and drove into Paignton to post them. Then dinner and – I'm not ashamed to say it – reread a book of E. Nesbit's that I used to love as a kid. Then the telephone rang –'

'No further. Now reflect, Mr Clarke, did you meet anyone on your way down to the sea in the morning?'

'Lots of people.'

'Can you remember anything about them?'

'Not a damned thing now.'

'Sure?'

'Well – let's see – I remember a remarkably fat woman – she wore a striped silk dress and I wondered why – had a couple of kids with her – two young men with a fox terrier on the beach throwing stones for it – Oh, yes, a girl with yellow hair squeaking as she bathed – funny how things come back – like a photograph developing.'

'You are a good subject. Now later in the day – the garden – going to the post –'

'The gardener watering . . . Going to the post? Nearly ran down a bicyclist – silly woman wobbling and shouting to a friend. That's all, I'm afraid.'

Poirot turned to Thora Grey.

'Miss Grey?'

Thora Grey replied in her clear, positive voice:

'I did correspondence with Sir Carmichael in the morning – saw the housekeeper. I wrote letters and did needlework in the afternoon, I fancy. It is difficult to remember. It was quite an ordinary day. I went to bed early.'

Rather to my surprise, Poirot asked no further. He said:

'Miss Barnard – can you bring back your remembrances of the last time you saw your sister?'

'It would be about a fortnight before her death. I was down for Saturday and Sunday. It was fine weather. We went to Hastings to the swimming pool.'

'What did you talk about most of the time?'

'I gave her a piece of my mind,' said Megan.

'And what else? She conversed of what?'

The girl frowned in an effort of memory.

'She talked about being hard up – of a hat and a couple of summer frocks she'd just bought. And a little of Don . . . She also said she disliked Milly Higley – that's the girl at the café – and we laughed about the Merrion woman who keeps the café . . . I don't remember anything else . . .'

'She didn't mention any man – forgive me, Mr Fraser – she might be meeting?'

'She wouldn't to me,' said Megan dryly.

Poirot turned to the red-haired young man with the square jaw.

'Mr Fraser – I want you to cast your mind back. You went, you said, to the café on the fatal evening. Your first intention was to wait there and watch for Betty Barnard to come out. Can you remember anyone at all whom you noticed whilst you were waiting there?'

'There were a large number of people walking along the front. I can't remember any of them.'

'Excuse me, but are you trying? However preoccupied the mind may be, the eye notices mechanically – unintelligently but accurately . . .'

The young man repeated doggedly:

'I don't remember anybody.'

Poirot sighed and turned to Mary Drower.

'I suppose you got letters from your aunt?'

'Oh, yes, sir.'

'When was the last?'

Mary thought a minute.

'Two days before the murder, sir.'

'What did it say?'

'She said the old devil had been round and that she'd sent him off with a flea in the ear – excuse the expression, sir – said she expected me over on the Wednesday – that's my day out, sir – and she said we'd go to the pictures. It was going to be my birthday, sir.'

Something – the thought of the little festivity perhaps – suddenly brought the tears to Mary's eyes. She gulped down a sob. Then apologized for it.

'You must forgive me, sir. I don't want to be silly. Crying's no good. It was just the thought of her – and me – looking forward to our treat. It upset me somehow, sir.'

'I know just what you feel like,' said Franklin Clarke. 'It's always the little things that get one – and especially anything like a treat or a present – something jolly and natural. I remember seeing a woman run over once. She'd just bought some new shoes. I saw her lying there – and the burst parcel with the ridiculous little high-heeled slippers peeping out – it gave me a turn – they looked so pathetic.'

Megan said with a sudden eager warmth:

'That's true – that's awfully true. The same thing happened after Betty – died. Mum had bought some stockings for her as a present – bought them the very day it happened. Poor mum, she was all broken up. I found her crying over them. She kept saying: "I bought them for Betty – I bought them for Betty – and she never even saw them."'

Her own voice quivered a little. She leaned forward, looking straight at Franklin Clarke. There was between them a sudden sympathy – a fraternity in trouble.

'I know,' he said. 'I know exactly. Those are just the sort of things that are hell to remember.'

Donald Fraser stirred uneasily.

Thora Grey diverted the conversation.

'Aren't we going to make any plans – for the future?' she asked.

'Of course.' Franklin Clarke resumed his ordinary manner. 'I think that when the moment comes – that is, when the fourth letter arrives – we ought to join forces. Until then, perhaps we might each try our luck on our own. I don't know whether there are any points M. Poirot thinks might repay investigation?'

'I could make some suggestions,' said Poirot.

'Good. I'll take them down.' He produced a notebook. 'Go ahead, M. Poirot. A –?'

'I consider it just possible that the waitress, Milly Higley, might know something useful.'

'A – Milly Higley,' wrote down Franklin Clarke.

'I suggest two methods of approach. You, Miss Barnard, might try what I call the offensive approach.'

'I suppose you think that suits my style?' said Megan dryly.

'Pick a quarrel with the girl – say you knew she never liked your sister – and that your sister had told you all about *her*. If I do not err, that will provoke a flood of recrimination. She will tell you just what she thought of your sister! Some useful fact may emerge.'

'And the second method?'

'May I suggest, Mr Fraser, that you should show signs of interest in the girl?'

'Is that necessary.'

'No, it is not necessary. It is just a possible line of exploration.'

'Shall I try my hand?' asked Franklin. 'I've – er – a

pretty wide experience, M. Poirot. Let me see what I can do with the young lady.'

'You've got your own part of the world to attend to,' said Thora Grey rather sharply.

Franklin's face fell just a little.

'Yes,' he said. 'I have.'

'*Tout de même*, I do not think there is much you can do down there for the present,' said Poirot. 'Mademoiselle Grey now, she is far more fitted –'

Thora Grey interrupted him.

'But you see, M. Poirot, I have left Devon for good.'

'Ah? I did not understand.'

'Miss Grey very kindly stayed on to help me clear up things,' said Franklin. 'But naturally she prefers a post in London.'

Poirot directed a sharp glance from one to the other.

'How is Lady Clarke?' he demanded.

I was admiring the faint colour in Thora Grey's cheeks and almost missed Clarke's reply.

'Pretty bad. By the way, M. Poirot, I wonder if you could see your way to running down to Devon and paying her a visit? She expressed a desire to see you before I left. Of course, she often can't see people for a couple of days at a time, but if you would risk that – at my expense, of course.'

'Certainly, Mr Clarke. Shall we say the day after tomorrow?'

'Good. I'll let nurse know and she'll arrange the dope accordingly.'

'For you, my child,' said Poirot, turning to Mary, 'I think you might perhaps do good work in Andover. Try the children.'

'The children?'

'Yes. Children will not chat readily to outsiders. But you are known in the street where your aunt lived. There were a good many children playing about. They may have noticed who went in and out of your aunt's shop.'

'What about Miss Grey and myself?' asked Clarke. 'That is, if I'm not to go to Bexhill.'

'M. Poirot,' said Thora Grey, 'what was the postmark on the third letter?'

'Putney, mademoiselle.'

She said thoughtfully: 'SW15, Putney, that is right, is it not?'

'For a wonder, the newspapers printed it correctly.'

'That seems to point to A B C being a Londoner.'

'On the face of it, yes.'

'One ought to be able to draw him,' said Clarke. 'M. Poirot, how would it be if I inserted an advertisement – something after these lines: *A B C. Urgent, H.P. close on your track. A hundred for my silence. X.Y.Z.* Nothing quite so crude as that – but you see the idea. It might draw him.'

'It is a possibility – yes.'

'Might induce him to try and have a shot at me.'

'I think it's very dangerous and silly,' said Thora Grey sharply.

'What about it, M. Poirot?'

'It can do no harm to try. I think myself that A B C will be too cunning to reply.' Poirot smiled a little. 'I see, Mr Clarke, that you are – if I may say so without being offensive – still a boy at heart.'

Franklin Clarke looked a little abashed.

'Well,' he said, consulting his notebook. 'We're making a start.

A – Miss Barnard and Milly Higley.

B – Mr Fraser and Miss Higley.

C – Children in Andover.

D – Advertisement.

'I don't feel any of it is much good, but it will be something to do whilst waiting.'

He got up and a few minutes later the meeting had dispersed.

Chapter 19

By Way of Sweden

Poirot returned to his seat and sat humming a little tune to himself.

'Unfortunate that she is so intelligent,' he murmured.

'Who?'

'Megan Barnard. Mademoiselle Megan. "Words," she snaps out. At once she perceives that what I am saying means nothing at all. Everybody else was taken in.'

'I thought it sounded very plausible.'

'Plausible, yes. It was just that she perceived.'

'Didn't you mean what you said, then?'

'What I said could have been comprised into one short sentence. Instead I repeated myself *ad lib* without anyone but Mademoiselle Megan being aware of the fact.'

'But why?'

'*Eh bien* – to get things going! To imbue everyone with the impression that there was work to be done! To start – shall we say – the conversations!'

'Don't you think any of these lines will lead to anything?'

'Oh, it is always possible.'

He chuckled.

'In the midst of tragedy we start the comedy. It is so, is it not?'

'What *do* you mean?'

'The human drama, Hastings! Reflect a little minute. Here are three sets of human beings brought together by a common tragedy. Immediately a second drama commences – *tout à fait à part.* Do you remember my first case in England? Oh, so many years ago now. I brought together two people who loved one another – by the simple method of having one of them arrested for murder! Nothing less would have done it! In the midst of death we are in life, Hastings . . . Murder, I have often noticed, is a great matchmaker.'

'Really, Poirot,' I cried scandalized. 'I'm sure none of those people was thinking of anything but –'

'Oh! my dear friend. And what about yourself?'

'I?'

'*Mais oui*, as they departed, did you not come back from the door humming a tune?'

'One may do that without being callous.'

'Certainly, but that tune told me your thoughts.'

'Indeed?'

'Yes. To hum a tune is extremely dangerous. It reveals the subconscious mind. The tune you hummed dates, I think, from the days of the war. *Comme ça*,' Poirot sang in an abominable falsetto voice:

'Some of the time I love a brunette,
Some of the time I love a blonde
(Who comes from Eden by way of Sweden).

'What could be more revealing? *Mais je crois que la blonde l'emporte sur la brunette!*'

'Really, Poirot,' I cried, blushing slightly.

'*C'est tout naturel.* Did you observe how Franklin Clarke was suddenly at one and in sympathy with Mademoiselle Megan? How he leaned forward and looked at her? And did you also notice how very much annoyed Mademoiselle Thora Grey was about it? And Mr Donald Fraser, he –'

'Poirot,' I said. 'Your mind is incurably sentimental.'

'That is the last thing my mind is. You are the sentimental one, Hastings.'

I was about to argue the point hotly, but at that moment the door opened.

To my astonishment it was Thora Grey who entered.

'Forgive me for coming back,' she said composedly.

'But there was something that I think I would like to tell you, M. Poirot.'

'Certainly, mademoiselle. Sit down, will you not?'

She took a seat and hesitated for just a minute as though choosing her words.

'It is just this, M. Poirot. Mr Clarke very generously gave you to understand just now that I had left Combeside by my own wish. He is a very kind and loyal person. But as a matter of fact, it is not quite like that. I was quite prepared to stay on – there is any amount of work to be done in connection with the collections. It was Lady Clarke who wished me to leave! I can make allowances. She is a very ill woman, and her brain is somewhat muddled with the drugs they give her. It makes her suspicious and fanciful. She took an unreasoning dislike to me and insisted that I should leave the house.'

I could not but admire the girl's courage. She did not attempt to gloss over facts, as so many might have been tempted to do, but went straight to the point with an admirable candour. My heart went out to her in admiration and sympathy.

'I call it splendid of you to come and tell us this,' I said.

'It's always better to have the truth,' she said with a little smile. 'I don't want to shelter behind Mr Clarke's chivalry. He is a very chivalrous man.'

There was a warm glow in her words. She evidently admired Franklin Clarke enormously.

'You have been very honest, mademoiselle,' said Poirot.

'It is rather a blow to me,' said Thora ruefully. 'I had no idea Lady Clarke disliked me so much. In fact, I always thought she was rather fond of me.' She made a wry face. 'One lives and learns.'

She rose.

'That is all I came to say. Goodbye.'

I accompanied her downstairs.

'I call that very sporting of her,' I said as I returned to the room. 'She has courage, that girl.'

'And calculation.'

'What do you mean – calculation?'

'I mean that she has the power of looking ahead.'

I looked at him doubtfully.

'She really is a lovely girl,' I said.

'And wears very lovely clothes. That crêpe marocain and the silver fox collar – *dernier cri*.'

'You're a man milliner, Poirot. I never notice what people have on.'

'You should join a nudist colony.'

As I was about to make an indignant rejoinder, he said, with a sudden change of subject:

'Do you know, Hastings, I cannot rid my mind of the impression that already, in our conversations this afternoon, something was said that was significant. It is odd – I cannot pin down exactly what it was . . . Just an impression that passed through my mind . . . *That reminds me of something I have already heard or seen or noted . . .*'

'Something at Churston?'

'No – not at Churston . . . Before that . . . No matter, presently it will come to me . . .'

He looked at me (perhaps I had not been attending very closely), laughed and began once more to hum.

'She is an angel, is she not? From Eden, by way of Sweden . . .'

'Poirot,' I said. 'Go to the devil!'

Chapter 20

Lady Clarke

There was an air of deep and settled melancholy over Combeside when we saw it again for the second time. This may, perhaps, have been partly due to the weather – it was a moist September day with a hint of autumn in the air, and partly, no doubt, it was the semi-shut-up state of the house. The downstairs rooms were closed and shuttered, and the small room into which we were shown smelt damp and airless.

A capable-looking hospital nurse came to us there pulling down her starched cuffs.

'M. Poirot?' she said briskly. 'I am Nurse Capstick. I got Mr Clarke's letter saying you were coming.'

Poirot inquired after Lady Clarke's health.

'Not at all bad really, all things considered.'

'All things considered,' I presumed, meant considering she was under sentence of death.

'One can't hope for much improvement, of course,

but some new treatment has made things a little easier for her. Dr Logan is quite pleased with her condition.'

'But it is true, is it not, that she can never recover?'

'Oh, we never actually *say* that,' said Nurse Capstick, a little shocked by this plain speaking.

'I suppose her husband's death was a terrible shock to her?'

'Well, M. Poirot, if you understand what I mean, it wasn't as much of a shock as it would have been to anyone in full possession of her health and faculties. Things are *dimmed* for Lady Clarke in her condition.'

'Pardon my asking, but was she deeply attached to her husband and he to her?'

'Oh, yes, they were a very happy couple. He was very worried and upset about her, poor man. It's always worse for a doctor, you know. They can't buoy themselves up with false hopes. I'm afraid it preyed on his mind very much to begin with.'

'To begin with? Not so much afterwards?'

'One gets used to everything, doesn't one? And then Sir Carmichael had his collection. A hobby is a great consolation to a man. He used to run up to sales occasionally, and then he and Miss Grey were busy recataloguing and rearranging the museum on a new system.'

'Oh, yes – Miss Grey. She has left, has she not?'

'Yes – I'm very sorry about it – but ladies do take

these fancies sometimes when they're not well. And there's no arguing with them. It's better to give in. Miss Grey was very sensible about it.'

'Had Lady Clarke always disliked her?'

'No – that is to say, not *disliked.* As a matter of fact, I think she rather liked her to begin with. But there, I mustn't keep you gossiping. My patient will be wondering what has become of us.'

She led us upstairs to a room on the first floor. What had at one time been a bedroom had been turned into a cheerful-looking sitting-room.

Lady Clarke was sitting in a big armchair near the window. She was painfully thin, and her face had the grey, haggard look of one who suffers much pain. She had a slightly faraway, dreamy look, and I noticed that the pupils of her eyes were mere pin-points.

'This is M. Poirot whom you wanted to see,' said Nurse Capstick in her high, cheerful voice.

'Oh, yes, M. Poirot,' said Lady Clarke vaguely.

She extended her hand.

'My friend Captain Hastings, Lady Clarke.'

'How do you do? So good of you both to come.'

We sat down as her vague gesture directed. There was a silence. Lady Clarke seemed to have lapsed into a dream.

Presently with a slight effort she roused herself.

'It was about Car, wasn't it? About Car's death. Oh, yes.'

She sighed, but still in a faraway manner, shaking her head.

'We never thought it would be that way round . . . I was so sure I should be the first to go . . .' She mused a minute or two. 'Car was very strong – wonderful for his age. He was never ill. He was nearly sixty – but he seemed more like fifty . . . Yes, very strong . . .'

She relapsed again into her dream. Poirot, who was well acquainted with the effects of certain drugs and of how they give their taker the impression of endless time, said nothing.

Lady Clarke said suddenly:

'Yes – it was good of you to come. I told Franklin. He said he wouldn't forget to tell you. I hope Franklin isn't going to be foolish . . . he's so easily taken in, in spite of having knocked about the world so much. Men are like that . . . They remain boys . . . Franklin, in particular.'

'He has an impulsive nature,' said Poirot.

'Yes – yes . . . And very chivalrous. Men are so foolish that way. Even Car –' Her voice tailed off.

She shook her head with a febrile impatience.

'Everything's so dim . . . One's body is a nuisance, M. Poirot, especially when it gets the upper hand. One is conscious of nothing else – whether the pain will hold off or not – nothing else seems to matter.'

'I know, Lady Clarke. It is one of the tragedies of this life.'

'It makes me so stupid. I cannot even remember what it was I wanted to say to you.'

'Was it something about your husband's death?'

'Car's death? Yes, perhaps . . . Mad, poor creature – the murderer, I mean. It's all the noise and the speed nowadays – people can't stand it. I've always been sorry for mad people – their heads must feel so queer. And then, being shut up – it must be so terrible. But what else can one do? If they kill people . . .' She shook her head – gently pained. 'You haven't caught him yet?' she asked.

'No, not yet.'

'He must have been hanging round here that day.'

'There were so many strangers about, Lady Clarke. It is the holiday season.'

'Yes – I forgot . . . But they keep down by the beaches, they don't come up near the house.'

'No stranger came to the house that day.'

'Who says so?' demanded Lady Clarke, with a sudden vigour.

Poirot looked slightly taken aback.

'The servants,' he said. 'Miss Grey.'

Lady Clarke said very distinctly:

'That girl is a liar!'

I started on my chair. Poirot threw me a glance.

Lady Clarke was going on, speaking now rather feverishly.

'I didn't like her. I never liked her. Car thought all the world of her. Used to go on about her being an orphan and alone in the world. What's wrong with being an orphan? Sometimes it's a blessing in disguise. You might have a good-for-nothing father and a mother who drank – then you would have something to complain about. Said she was so brave and such a good worker. I dare say she did her work well! I don't know where all this bravery came in!'

'Now don't excite yourself, dear,' said Nurse Capstick, intervening. 'We mustn't have you getting tired.'

'I soon sent her packing! Franklin had the impertinence to suggest that she might be a comfort to me. Comfort to me indeed! The sooner I saw the last of her the better – that's what I said! Franklin's a fool! I didn't want him getting mixed up with her. He's a boy! No sense! "I'll give her three months' salary, if you like," I said. "But out she goes. I don't want her in the house a day longer." There's one thing about being ill – men can't argue with you. He did what I said and she went. Went like a martyr, I expect – with more sweetness and bravery!'

'Now, dear, don't get so excited. It's bad for you.'

Lady Clarke waved Nurse Capstick away.

'You were as much of a fool about her as anyone else.'

'Oh! Lady Clarke, you mustn't say that. I did think

Miss Grey a very nice girl – so romantic-looking, like someone out of a novel.'

'I've no patience with the lot of you,' said Lady Clarke feebly.

'Well, she's gone now, my dear. Gone right away.'

Lady Clarke shook her head with feeble impatience but she did not answer.

Poirot said:

'Why did you say that Miss Grey was a liar?'

'Because she is. She told you no strangers came to the house, didn't she?'

'Yes.'

'Very well, then. I saw her – with my own eyes – out of this window – talking to a perfectly strange man on the front doorstep.'

'When was this?'

'In the morning of the day Car died – about eleven o'clock.'

'What did this man look like?'

'An ordinary sort of man. Nothing special.'

'A gentleman – or a tradesman?'

'Not a tradesman. A shabby sort of person. I can't remember.'

A sudden quiver of pain shot across her face.

'Please – you must go now – I'm a little tired – Nurse.'

We obeyed the cue and took our departure.

'That's an extraordinary story,' I said to Poirot as

we journeyed back to London. 'About Miss Grey and a strange man.'

'You see, Hastings? It is, as I tell you: *there is always something to be found out.*'

'Why did the girl lie about it and say she had seen no one?'

'I can think of seven separate reasons – one of them an extremely simple one.'

'Is that a snub?' I asked.

'It is, perhaps, an invitation to use your ingenuity. But there is no need for us to perturb ourselves. The easiest way to answer the question is to ask her.'

'And suppose she tells us another lie.'

'That would indeed be interesting – and highly suggestive.'

'It is monstrous to suppose that a girl like that could be in league with a madman.'

'Precisely – so I do not suppose it.'

I thought for some minutes longer.

'A good-looking girl has a hard time of it,' I said at last with a sigh.

'*Du tout*. Disabuse your mind of that idea.'

'It's true,' I insisted, 'everyone's hand is against her simply because she is good-looking.'

'You speak the *bêtises*, my friend. Whose hand was against her at Combeside? Sir Carmichael's? Franklin's? Nurse Capstick's?'

'Lady Clarke was down on her, all right.'

'*Mon ami*, you are full of charitable feeling towards beautiful young girls. Me, I feel charitable to sick old ladies. It may be that Lady Clarke was the clear-sighted one – and that her husband, Mr Franklin Clarke and Nurse Capstick were all as blind as bats – and Captain Hastings.'

'You've got a grudge against that girl, Poirot.'

To my surprise his eyes twinkled suddenly.

'Perhaps it is that I like to mount you on your romantic high horse, Hastings. You are always the true knight – ready to come to the rescue of damsels in distress – good-looking damsels, *bien entendu*.'

'How ridiculous you are, Poirot,' I said, unable to keep from laughing.

'Ah, well, one cannot be tragic all the time. More and more I interest myself in the human developments that arise out of this tragedy. It is three dramas of family life that we have there. First there is Andover – the whole tragic life of Mrs Ascher, her struggles, her support of her German husband, the devotion of her niece. That alone would make a novel. Then you have Bexhill – the happy, easy-going father and mother, the two daughters so widely differing from each other – the pretty fluffy fool, and the intense, strong-willed Megan with her clear intelligence and her ruthless passion for truth. And the other figure –

the self-controlled young Scotsman with his passionate jealousy and his worship of the dead girl. Finally you have the Churston household – the dying wife, and the husband absorbed in his collections, but with a growing tenderness and sympathy for the beautiful girl who helps him so sympathetically, and then the younger brother, vigorous, attractive, interesting, with a romantic glamour about him from his long travels.

'Realize, Hastings, that in the ordinary course of events *those three separate dramas would never have touched each other*. They would have pursued their course uninfluenced by each other. The permutations and combinations of life, Hastings – I never cease to be fascinated by them.'

'This is Paddington,' was the only answer I made.

It was time, I felt, that someone pricked the bubble.

On our arrival at Whitehaven Mansions we were told that a gentleman was waiting to see Poirot.

I expected it to be Franklin, or perhaps Japp, but to my astonishment it turned out to be none other than Donald Fraser.

He seemed very embarrassed and his inarticulateness was more noticeable than ever.

Poirot did not press him to come to the point of his visit, but instead suggested sandwiches and a glass of wine.

Until these made their appearance he monopolized

the conversation, explaining where we had been, and speaking with kindliness and feeling of the invalid woman.

Not until we had finished the sandwiches and sipped the wine did he give the conversation a personal turn.

'You have come from Bexhill, Mr Fraser?'

'Yes.'

'Any success with Milly Higley?'

'Milly Higley? Milly Higley?' Fraser repeated the name wonderingly. 'Oh, that girl! No, I haven't done anything there yet. It's –'

He stopped. His hands twisted themselves together nervously.

'I don't know why I've come to you,' he burst out.

'I know,' said Poirot.

'You can't. How can you?'

'You have come to me because there is something that you must tell to someone. You were quite right. I am the proper person. Speak!'

Poirot's air of assurance had its effect. Fraser looked at him with a queer air of grateful obedience.

'You think so?'

'*Parbleu*, I am sure of it.'

'M. Poirot, do you know anything about dreams?'

It was the last thing I had expected him to say.

Poirot, however, seemed in no wise surprised.

'I do,' he replied. 'You have been dreaming –?'

'Yes. I suppose you'll say it's only natural that I should – should dream about – It. But it isn't an ordinary dream.'

'No?'

'No?'

'I've dreamed it now three nights running, sir . . . I think I'm going mad . . .'

'Tell me –'

The man's face was livid. His eyes were staring out of his head. As a matter of fact, he *looked* mad.

'It's always the same. I'm on the beach. Looking for Betty. She's lost – only lost, you understand. I've got to find her. I've got to give her her belt. I'm carrying it in my hand. And then –'

'Yes?'

'The dream changes . . . I'm not looking any more. She's there in front of me – sitting on the beach. She doesn't see me coming – It's – oh, I can't –'

'Go on.'

Poirot's voice was authoritative – firm.

'I come up behind her . . . she doesn't hear me . . . I slip the belt round her neck and pull – oh – pull . . .'

The agony in his voice was frightful . . . I gripped the arms of my chair . . . The thing was too real.

'She's choking . . . she's dead . . . I've strangled her – and then her head falls back and I see her face . . . and it's *Megan* – not Betty!'

He leant back white and shaking. Poirot poured out another glass of wine and passed it over to him.

'What's the meaning of it, M. Poirot? Why does it come to me? Every night . . . ?'

'Drink up your wine,' ordered Poirot.

The young man did so, then he asked in a calmer voice:

'What does it mean? I – I didn't kill her, did I?'

What Poirot answered I do not know, for at that minute I heard the postman's knock and automatically I left the room.

What I took out of the letter-box banished all my interest in Donald Fraser's extraordinary revelations.

I raced back into the sitting-room.

'Poirot,' I cried. 'It's come. The fourth letter.'

He sprang up, seized it from me, caught up his paper-knife and slit it open. He spread it out on the table.

The three of us read it together.

Still no success? Fie! Fie! What are you and the police doing? Well, well, isn't this fun? And where shall we go next for honey?

Poor Mr Poirot. I'm quite sorry for you.

If at first you don't succeed, try, try, try again.

We've a long way to go still.

Tipperary? No – that comes farther on. Letter T.

The next little incident will take place at Doncaster on September 11th.

So long.

A B C.

Chapter 21

Description of a Murderer

It was at this moment, I think, that what Poirot called the human element began to fade out of the picture again. It was as though, the mind being unable to stand unadulterated horror, we had had an interval of normal human interests.

We had, one and all, felt the impossibility of doing anything until the fourth letter should come revealing the projected scene of the D murder. That atmosphere of waiting had brought a release of tension.

But now, with the printed words jeering from the white stiff paper, the hunt was up once more.

Inspector Crome had come round from the Yard, and while he was still there, Franklin Clarke and Megan Barnard came in.

The girl explained that she, too, had come up from Bexhill.

'I wanted to ask Mr Clarke something.'

She seemed rather anxious to excuse and explain her procedure. I just noted the fact without attaching much importance to it.

The letter naturally filled my mind to the exclusion of all else.

Crome was not, I think, any too pleased to see the various participants in the drama. He became extremely official and non-committal.

'I'll take this with me, M. Poirot. If you care to take a copy of it –'

'No, no, it is not necessary.'

'What are your plans, inspector?' asked Clarke.

'Fairly comprehensive ones, Mr Clarke.'

'This time we've got to get him,' said Clarke. 'I may tell you, inspector, that we've formed an association of our own to deal with the matter. A legion of interested parties.'

Inspector Crome said in his best manner:

'Oh, yes?'

'I gather you don't think much of amateurs, inspector?'

'You've hardly the same resources at your command, have you, Mr Clarke?'

'We've got a personal axe to grind – and that's something.'

'Oh, yes?'

'I fancy your own task isn't going to be too easy,

inspector. In fact, I rather fancy old A B C has done you again.'

Crome, I noticed, could often be goaded into speech when other methods would have failed.

'I don't fancy the public will have much to criticize in our arrangements this time,' he said. 'The fool has given us ample warning. The 11th isn't till Wednesday of next week. That gives ample time for a publicity campaign in the press. Doncaster will be thoroughly warned. Every soul whose name begins with a D will be on his or her guard – that's so much to the good. Also, we'll draft police into the town on a fairly large scale. That's already been arranged for by consent of all the Chief Constables in England. The whole of Doncaster, police and civilians, will be out to catch one man – and with reasonable luck, we ought to get him!'

Clarke said quietly:

'It's easy to see you're not a sporting man, inspector.'

Crome stared at him.

'What do you mean, Mr Clarke?'

'Man alive, don't you realize that on *next Wednesday the St Leger is being run at Doncaster?*'

The inspector's jaw dropped. For the life of him he could not bring out the familiar 'Oh, yes?' Instead he said:

'That's true. Yes, that complicates matters . . .'

'A B C is no fool, even if he *is* a madman.'

We were all silent for a minute or two, taking in the situation. The crowds on the race-course – the passionate, sport-loving English public – the endless complications.

Poirot murmured:

'*C'est ingénieux. Tout de même c'est bien imaginé, ça.*'

'It's my belief,' said Clarke, 'that the murder will take place on the race-course – perhaps actually while the Leger is being run.'

For the moment his sporting instincts took a momentary pleasure in the thought . . .

Inspector Crome rose, taking the letter with him.

'The St Leger is a complication,' he allowed. 'It's unfortunate.'

He went out. We heard a murmur of voices in the hallway. A minute later Thora Grey entered.

She said anxiously:

'The inspector told me there is another letter. Where this time?'

It was raining outside. Thora Grey was wearing a black coat and skirt and furs. A little black hat just perched itself on the side of her golden head.

It was to Franklin Clarke that she spoke and she came right up to him and, with a hand on his arm, waited for his answer.

'Doncaster – and on the day of the St Leger.'

We settled down to a discussion. It went without saying that we all intended to be present, but the race-meeting undoubtedly complicated the plans we had made tentatively beforehand.

A feeling of discouragement swept over me. What could this little band of six people do, after all, however strong their personal interest in the matter might be? There would be innumerable police, keen-eyed and alert, watching all likely spots. What could six more pairs of eyes do?

As though in answer to my thought, Poirot raised his voice. He spoke rather like a schoolmaster or a priest.

'*Mes enfants*,' he said. 'We must not disperse the strength. We must approach this matter with method and order in our thoughts. We must look within and not without for the truth. We must say to ourselves – each one of us – what do *I* know about the murderer? And so we must build up a composite picture of the man we are going to seek.'

'We know nothing about him,' sighed Thora Grey helplessly.

'No, no, mademoiselle. That is not true. Each one of us knows something about him – *if we only knew what it is we know. I am convinced that the knowledge is there* if we could only get at it.'

Clarke shook his head.

'We don't know anything – whether he's old or

young, fair or dark! None of us has ever seen him or spoken to him! We've gone over everything we all know again and again.'

'Not everything! For instance, Miss Grey here told us that she did not see or speak to any stranger on the day that Sir Carmichael Clarke was murdered.'

Thora Grey nodded.

'That's quite right.'

'Is it? *Lady Clarke told us, mademoiselle, that from her window she saw you standing on the front doorstep talking to a man.*'

'She saw *me* talking to a strange man?' The girl seemed genuinely astonished. Surely that pure, limpid look could not be anything but genuine.

She shook her head.

'Lady Clarke must have made a mistake. I never – Oh!'

The exclamation came suddenly – jerked out of her. A crimson wave flooded her cheeks.

'I remember now! How stupid! I'd forgotten all about it. But it wasn't important. Just one of those men who come round selling stockings – you know, ex-army people. They're very persistent. I had to get rid of him. I was just crossing the hall when he came to the door. He spoke to me instead of ringing but he was quite a harmless sort of person. I suppose that's why I forgot about him.'

Poirot was swaying to and fro, his hands clasped to his head. He was muttering to himself with such vehemence that nobody else said anything, but stared at him instead.

'Stockings,' he was murmuring. 'Stockings . . . stockings . . . stockings . . . *ça vient* . . . stockings . . . stockings . . . it is the *motif* – *yes* . . . three months ago . . . and the other day . . . and now. *Bon Dieu*, I have it!'

He sat upright and fixed me with an imperious eye.

'You remember, Hastings? Andover. The shop. We go upstairs. The bedroom. On a chair. *A pair of new silk stockings.* And now I know what it was that roused my attention two days ago. It was you, mademoiselle–' He turned on Megan. 'You spoke of your mother who wept *because she had bought your sister some new stockings on the very day of the murder* . . .'

He looked round on us all.

'You see? *It is the same motif* three times repeated. That cannot be coincidence. When mademoiselle spoke I had the feeling that what she said linked up with something. I know now with what. The words spoken by Mrs Ascher's next-door neighbour, Mrs Fowler. About people who were always trying to *sell* you things – and she mentioned *stockings*. Tell me, mademoiselle, it is true, is it not, that your mother bought those stockings, not at a shop, but from someone who came to the door?'

'Yes – yes – she did . . . I remember now. She said something about being sorry for these wretched men who go round and try to get orders.'

'But what's the connection?' cried Franklin. 'That a man came selling stockings proves nothing!'

'I tell you, my friends, it *cannot* be coincidence. Three crimes – and every time a man selling stockings and spying out the land.'

He wheeled round on Thora.

'*A vous la parole!* Describe this man.'

She looked at him blankly.

'I can't . . . I don't know how . . . He had glasses, I think – and a shabby overcoat . . .'

'*Mieux que ça, mademoiselle.*'

'He stooped . . . I don't know. I hardly looked at him. He wasn't the sort of man you'd notice . . .'

Poirot said gravely:

'You are quite right, mademoiselle. The whole secret of the murders lies there in your description of the murderer – for without a doubt he *was* the murderer! "*He wasn't the sort of man you'd notice.*" Yes – there is no doubt about it . . . You have described the murderer!'

Chapter 22

Not from Captain Hastings' Personal Narrative

Mr Alexander Bonaparte Cust sat very still. His breakfast lay cold and untasted on his plate. A newspaper was propped up against the teapot and it was this newspaper that Mr Cust was reading with avid interest.

Suddenly he got up, paced to and fro for a minute, then sank back into a chair by the window. He buried his head in his hands with a stifled groan.

He did not hear the sound of the opening door. His landlady, Mrs Marbury, stood in the doorway.

'I was wondering, Mr Cust, if you'd fancy a nice – why, whatever is it? Aren't you feeling well?'

Mr Cust raised his head from his hands.

'Nothing. It's nothing at all, Mrs Marbury. I'm not – feeling very well this morning.'

Mrs Marbury inspected the breakfast tray.

'So I see. You haven't touched your breakfast. Is it your head troubling you again?'

'No. At least, yes . . . I – I just feel a bit out of sorts.'

'Well, I'm sorry, I'm sure. You'll not be going away today, then?'

Mr Cust sprang up abruptly.

'No, no. I have to go. It's business. Important. Very important.'

His hands were shaking. Seeing him so agitated, Mrs Marbury tried to soothe him.

'Well, if you must – you must. Going far this time?'

'No. I'm going to' – he hesitated for a minute or two – 'Cheltenham.'

There was something so peculiar about the tentative way he said the word that Mrs Marbury looked at him in surprise.

'Cheltenham's a nice place,' she said conversationally. 'I went there from Bristol one year. The shops are ever so nice.'

'I suppose so – yes.'

Mrs Marbury stooped rather stiffly – for stooping did not suit her figure – to pick up the paper that was lying crumpled on the floor.

'Nothing but this murdering business in the papers nowadays,' she said as she glanced at the headlines before putting it back on the table. 'Gives me the creeps, it does. I don't read it. It's like Jack the Ripper all over again.'

Mr Cust's lips moved, but no sound came from them.

'Doncaster – that's the place he's going to do his next murder,' said Mrs Marbury. 'And tomorrow! Fairly makes your flesh creep, doesn't it? If I lived in Doncaster and my name began with a D, I'd take the first train away, that I would. I'd run no risks. What did you say, Mr Cust?'

'Nothing, Mrs Marbury – nothing.'

'It's the races and all. No doubt he thinks he'll get his opportunity there. Hundreds of police, they say, they're drafting in and – Why, Mr Cust, you *do* look bad. Hadn't you better have a little drop of something? Really, now, you oughtn't to go travelling today.'

Mr Cust drew himself up.

'It is necessary, Mrs Marbury. I have always been punctual in my – engagements. People must have – must have confidence in you! When I have undertaken to do a thing, I carry it through. It is the only way to get on in – in – business.'

'But if you're ill?'

'I am not ill, Mrs Marbury. Just a little worried over – various personal matters. I slept badly. I am really quite all right.'

His manner was so firm that Mrs Marbury gathered

up the breakfast things and reluctantly left the room.

Mr Cust dragged out a suitcase from under the bed and began to pack. Pyjamas, sponge-bag, spare collar, leather slippers. Then unlocking a cupboard, he transferred a dozen or so flattish cardboard boxes about ten inches by seven from a shelf to the suitcase.

He just glanced at the railway guide on the table and then left the room, suitcase in hand.

Setting it down in the hall, he put on his hat and overcoat. As he did so he sighed deeply, so deeply that the girl who came out from a room at the side looked at him in concern.

'Anything the matter, Mr Cust?'

'Nothing, Miss Lily.'

'You were sighing so!'

Mr Cust said abruptly:

'Are you at all subject to premonitions, Miss Lily? To presentiments?'

'Well, I don't know that I am, really . . . Of course, there are days when you just feel everything's going wrong, and days when you feel everything's going right.'

'Quite,' said Mr Cust.

He sighed again.

'Well, goodbye, Miss Lily. Goodbye. I'm sure you've been very kind to me always here.'

'Well, don't say goodbye as though you were going away for ever,' laughed Lily.

'No, no, of course not.'

'See you Friday,' laughed the girl. 'Where are you going this time? Seaside again.'

'No, no – er – Cheltenham.'

'Well, that's nice, too. But not quite as nice as Torquay. That must have been lovely. I want to go there for my holiday next year. By the way, you must have been quite near where the murder was – the A B C murder. It happened while you were down there, didn't it?'

'Er – yes. But Churston's six or seven miles away.'

'All the same, it must have been exciting! Why, you may have passed the murderer in the street! You may have been quite near to him!'

'Yes, I may, of course,' said Mr Cust with such a ghastly and contorted smile that Lily Marbury noticed it.

'Oh, Mr Cust, you *don't* look well.'

'I'm quite all right, quite all right. Goodbye, Miss Marbury.'

He fumbled to raise his hat, caught up his suitcase and fairly hastened out of the front door.

'Funny old thing,' said Lily Marbury indulgently. 'Looks half batty to my mind.'

II

Inspector Crome said to his subordinate:

'Get me out a list of all stocking manufacturing firms and circularize them. I want a list of all their agents – you know, fellows who sell on commission and tout for orders.'

'This the A B C case, sir?'

'Yes. One of Mr Hercule Poirot's ideas.' The inspector's tone was disdainful. 'Probably nothing in it, but it doesn't do to neglect any chance, however faint.'

'Right, sir. Mr Poirot's done some good stuff in his time, but I think he's a bit gaga now, sir.'

'He's a mountebank,' said Inspector Crome. 'Always posing. Takes in some people. It doesn't take in *me*. Now then, about the arrangement for Doncaster . . .'

III

Tom Hartigan said to Lily Marbury:

'Saw your old dugout this morning.'

'Who? Mr Cust?'

'Cust it was. At Euston. Looking like a lost hen, as usual. I think the fellow's half loony. He needs someone to look after him. First he dropped his paper and then he dropped his ticket. I picked that up – he hadn't the faintest idea he'd lost it. Thanked me in an agitated sort of manner, but I don't think he recognized me.'

'Oh, well,' said Lily. 'He's only seen you passing in the hall, and not very often at that.'

They danced once round the floor.

'You dance something beautiful,' said Tom.

'Go on,' said Lily and wriggled yet a little closer.

They danced round again.

'Did you say Euston or Paddington?' asked Lily abruptly. 'Where you saw old Cust, I mean?'

'Euston.'

'Are you sure?'

'Of course I'm sure. What do you think?'

'Funny. I thought you went to Cheltenham from Paddington.'

'So you do. But old Cust wasn't going to Cheltenham. He was going to Doncaster.'

'Cheltenham.'

'Doncaster. I know, my girl! After all, I picked up his ticket, didn't I?'

'Well, he told *me* he was going to Cheltenham. I'm sure he did.'

'Oh, you've got it wrong. He was going to Doncaster all right. Some people have all the luck. I've got a bit on Firefly for the Leger and I'd love to see it run.'

'I shouldn't think Mr Cust went to race-meetings,

he doesn't look the kind. Oh, Tom, I hope he won't get murdered. It's Doncaster the A B C murder's going to be.'

'Cust'll be all right. His name doesn't begin with a D.'

'He might have been murdered last time. He was down near Churston at Torquay when the last murder happened.'

'Was he? That's a bit of a coincidence, isn't it?'

He laughed.

'He wasn't at Bexhill the time before, was he?'

Lily crinkled her brows.

'He was away . . . Yes, I remember he was away . . . because he forgot his bathing-dress. Mother was mending it for him. And she said: "There – Mr Cust went away yesterday without his bathing-dress after all," and I said: "Oh, never mind the old bathing-dress – there's been the most awful murder," I said, "a girl strangled at Bexhill."'

'Well, if he wanted his bathing-dress, he must have been going to the seaside. I say, Lily' – his face crinkled up with amusement. 'What price your old dugout being the murderer himself?'

'Poor Mr Cust? He wouldn't hurt a fly,' laughed Lily.

They danced on happily – in their conscious minds nothing but the pleasure of being together.

In their unconscious minds something stirred . . .

Chapter 23

September 11th. Doncaster

Doncaster!

I shall, I think, remember that 11th of September all my life.

Indeed, whenever I see a mention of the St Leger my mind flies automatically not to horse-racing but to murder.

When I recall my own sensations, the thing that stands out most is a sickening sense of insufficiency. We were here – on the spot – Poirot, myself, Clarke, Fraser, Megan Barnard, Thora Grey and Mary Drower, and in the last resort *what could any of us do?*

We were building on a forlorn hope – on the chance of recognizing amongst a crowd of thousands of people a face or figure imperfectly seen on an occasion one, two or three months back.

The odds were in reality greater than that. Of us all, the only person likely to make such a recognition was

Thora Grey.

Some of her serenity had broken down under the strain. Her calm, efficient manner was gone. She sat twisting her hands together, almost weeping, appealing incoherently to Poirot.

'I never really looked at him . . . Why didn't I? What a fool I was. You're depending on me, all of you . . . and I shall let you down. Because even if I did see him again I mightn't recognize him. I've got a bad memory for faces.'

Poirot, whatever he might say to me, and however harshly he might seem to criticize the girl, showed nothing but kindness now. His manner was tender in the extreme. It struck me that Poirot was no more indifferent to beauty in distress than I was.

He patted her shoulder kindly.

'Now then, *petite*, not the hysteria. We cannot have that. If you should see this man you would recognize him.'

'How do you know?'

'Oh, a great many reasons – for one, because the red succeeds the black.'

'What do you mean, Poirot?' I cried.

'I speak the language of the tables. At roulette there may be a long run on the black – but in the end *red must turn up*. It is the mathematical laws of chance.'

'You mean that luck turns?'

'Exactly, Hastings. And that is where the gambler

(and the murderer, who is, after all, only a supreme kind of gambler since what he risks is not his money but his life) often lacks intelligent anticipation. Because he *has* won he thinks he will *continue* to win! He does not leave the tables in good time with his pocket full. So in crime the murderer who is successful *cannot conceive the possibility of not being successful!* He takes to *himself* all the credit for a successful performance – but I tell you, my friends, however carefully planned, no crime can be successful without luck!'

'Isn't that going rather far?' demurred Franklin Clarke.

Poirot waved his hands excitedly.

'No, no. It is an even chance, if you like, but it *must* be in your favour. Consider! It might have happened that someone enters Mrs Ascher's shop just as the murderer is leaving. That person might have thought of looking behind the counter, have seen the dead woman – and either laid hands on the murderer straight away or else been able to give such an accurate description of him to the police that he would have been arrested forthwith.'

'Yes, of course, that's possible,' admitted Clarke. 'What it comes to is that a murderer's got to take a chance.'

'Precisely. A murderer is always a gambler. And, like many gamblers, a murderer often does not know when to stop. With each crime his opinion of his own abilities is strengthened. His sense of proportion is warped. He does not say "I have been clever *and lucky*!" No, he says only "I have been clever!" And his opinion of his cleverness grows and then, *mes amis*, the ball spins, and the run of colour is over – it drops into a new number and the croupier calls out "*Rouge*."'

'You think that will happen in this case?' asked Megan, drawing her brows together in a frown.

'It *must* happen sooner or later! So far *the luck has been with the criminal* – sooner or later it must turn and be with us. I believe that it *has* turned! The clue of the stockings is the beginning. Now, instead of everything going *right* for him, everything will go *wrong* for him! And he, too, will begin to make mistakes . . .'

'I will say you're heartening,' said Franklin Clarke. 'We all need a bit of comfort. I've had a paralysing feeling of helplessness ever since I woke up.'

'It seems to me highly problematical that we can accomplish anything of practical value,' said Donald Fraser.

Megan rapped out:

'Don't be a defeatist, Don.'

Mary Drower, flushing up a little, said:

'What I say is, you never know. That wicked fiend's in this place, and so are we – and after all, you do run up against people in the funniest way sometimes.'

I fumed:

'If only we could do something more.'

'You must remember, Hastings, that the police are doing everything reasonably possible. Special constables have been enrolled. The good Inspector Crome may have the irritating manner, but he is a very able police officer, and Colonel Anderson, the Chief Constable, is a man of action. They have taken the fullest measures for watching and patrolling the town and the race-course. There will be plain-clothes men everywhere. There is also the press campaign. The public is fully warned.'

Donald Fraser shook his head.

'He'll never attempt it, I'm thinking,' he said more hopefully. 'The man would just be mad!'

'Unfortunately,' said Clarke dryly, 'he is mad! What do you think, M. Poirot? Will he give it up or will he try to carry it through?'

'In my opinion the strength of his obsession is such that he *must* attempt to carry out his promise! Not to do so would be to admit failure, and that his insane egoism would never allow. That, I may say, is also Dr Thompson's opinion. Our hope is that he may be caught in the attempt.'

Donald shook his head again.

'He'll be very cunning.'

Poirot glanced at his watch. We took the hint. It had

been agreed that we were to make an all-day session of it, patrolling as many streets as possible in the morning, and later, stationing ourselves at various likely points on the race-course.

I say 'we'. Of course, in my own case such a patrol was of little avail since I was never likely to have set eyes on A B C. However, as the idea was to separate so as to cover as wide an area as possible I had suggested that I should act as escort to one of the ladies.

Poirot had agreed – I am afraid with somewhat of a twinkle in his eye.

The girls went off to get their hats on. Donald Fraser was standing by the window looking out, apparently lost in thought.

Franklin Clarke glanced over at him, then evidently deciding that the other was too abstracted to count as a listener, he lowered his voice a little and addressed Poirot.

'Look here, M. Poirot. You went down to Churston, I know, and saw my sister-in-law. Did she say – or hint – I mean – did she suggest at all –?'

He stopped, embarrassed.

Poirot answered with a face of blank innocence that aroused my strongest suspicions.

'*Comment?* Did your sister-in-law say, hint, or suggest – what?'

Franklin Clarke got rather red.

'Perhaps you think this isn't a time for butting in with personal things –'

'*Du tout!*'

'But I feel I'd like to get things quite straight.'

'An admirable course.'

This time I think Clarke began to suspect Poirot's bland face of concealing some inner amusement. He ploughed on rather heavily.

'My sister-in-law's an awfully nice woman – I've been very fond of her always – but of course she's been ill some time – and in that kind of illness – being given drugs and all that – one tends to – well, to *fancy* things about people!'

'Ah?'

By now there was no mistaking the twinkle in Poirot's eye.

But Franklin Clarke, absorbed in his diplomatic task, was past noticing it.

'It's about Thora – Miss Grey,' he said.

'Oh, it is of Miss Grey you speak?' Poirot's tone held innocent surprise.

'Yes. Lady Clarke got certain ideas in her head. You see, Thora – Miss Grey is well, rather a good-looking girl –'

'Perhaps – yes,' conceded Poirot.

'And women, even the best of them, are a bit catty about other women. Of course, Thora was invaluable to my brother – he always said she was the best secretary he ever had – and he was very fond of her, too. But it was all perfectly straight and above-board. I mean, Thora isn't the sort of girl –'

'No?' said Poirot helpfully.

'But my sister-in-law got it into her head to be – well – jealous, I suppose. Not that she ever showed anything. But after Car's death, when there was a question of Miss Grey staying on – well, Charlotte cut up rough. Of course, it's partly the illness and the morphia and all that – Nurse Capstick says so – she says we mustn't blame Charlotte for getting these ideas into her head –'

He paused.

'Yes?'

'What I want you to understand, M. Poirot, is that there isn't anything in it at all. It's just a sick woman's imaginings. Look here' – he fumbled in his pocket – 'here's a letter I received from my brother when I was in the Malay States. I'd like you to read it because it shows exactly what terms they were on.'

Poirot took it. Franklin came over beside him and with a pointing finger read some of the extracts out loud.

'– things go on here much as usual. Charlotte is moderately free from pain. I wish one could say more. You may remember Thora Grey? She is a dear girl and

a greater comfort to me than I can tell you. I should not have known what to do through this bad time but for her. Her sympathy and interest are unfailing. She has an exquisite taste and flair for beautiful things and shares my passion for Chinese art. I was indeed lucky to find her. No daughter could be a closer or more sympathetic companion. Her life had been a difficult and not always a happy one, but I am glad to feel that here she has a home and true affection.

'You see,' said Franklin, '*that's* how my brother felt to her. He thought of her like a daughter. What I feel so unfair is the fact that the moment my brother is dead, his wife practically turns her out of the house! Women really are devils, M. Poirot.'

'Your sister-in-law is ill and in pain, remember.'

'I know. That's what I keep saying to myself. One mustn't judge her. All the same, I thought I'd show you this. I don't want you to get a false impression of Thora from anything Lady Clarke may have said.'

Poirot returned the letter.

'I can assure you,' he said, smiling, 'that I never permit myself to get false impressions from anything anyone tells me. I form my own judgments.'

'Well,' said Clarke, stowing away the letter. 'I'm glad I showed it to you anyway. Here come the girls. We'd better be off.'

As we left the room, Poirot called me back.

'You are determined to accompany the expedition, Hastings?'

'Oh, yes. I shouldn't be happy staying here inactive.'

'There is activity of mind as well as body, Hastings.'

'Well, you're better at it than I am,' I said.

'You are incontestably right, Hastings. Am I correct in supposing that you intend to be a cavalier to one of the ladies?'

'That was the idea.'

'And which lady did you propose to honour with your company?'

'Well – I – er – hadn't considered yet.'

'What about Miss Barnard?'

'She's rather the independent type,' I demurred.

'Miss Grey?'

'Yes. She's better.'

'I find you, Hastings, singularly though transparently dishonest! All along you had made up your mind to spend the day with your blonde angel!'

'Oh, really, Poirot!'

'I am sorry to upset your plans, but I must request you to give your escort elsewhere.'

'Oh, all right. I think you've got a weakness for that Dutch doll of a girl.'

'The person you are to escort is Mary Drower – and I must request you not to leave her.'

'But, Poirot, why?'

'Because, my dear friend, her name begins with a D. We must take no chances.'

I saw the justice of his remark. At first it seemed far-fetched, but then I realized that if A B C had a fanatical hatred of Poirot, he might very well be keeping himself informed of Poirot's movements. And in that case the elimination of Mary Drower might strike him as a very pat fourth stroke.

I promised to be faithful to my trust.

I went out leaving Poirot sitting in a chair near the window.

In front of him was a little roulette wheel. He spun it as I went out of the door and called after me:

'*Rouge* – that is a good omen, Hastings. The luck, it turns!'

Chapter 24

Not from Captain Hastings' Personal Narrative

Below his breath Mr Leadbetter uttered a grunt of impatience as his next-door neighbour got up and stumbled clumsily past him, dropping his hat over the seat in front, and leaning over to retrieve it.

All this at the culminating moment of *Not a Sparrow*, that all-star, thrilling drama of pathos and beauty that Mr Leadbetter had been looking forward to seeing for a whole week.

The golden-haired heroine, played by Katherine Royal (in Mr Leadbetter's opinion the leading film actress in the world), was just giving vent to a hoarse cry of indignation:

'Never. I would sooner starve. But I shan't starve. Remember those words: *not a sparrow falls* –'

Mr Leadbetter moved his head irritably from right to left. People! Why on earth people couldn't wait till the *end* of a film . . . And to leave at this soul-stirring moment.

Ah, that was better. The annoying gentleman had passed on and out. Mr Leadbetter had a full view of the screen and of Katherine Royal standing by the window in the Van Schreiner Mansion in New York.

And now she was boarding the train – the child in her arms . . . What curious trains they had in America – not at all like English trains.

Ah, there was Steve again in his shack in the mountains . . .

The film pursued its course to its emotional and semi-religious end.

Mr Leadbetter breathed a sigh of satisfaction as the lights went up.

He rose slowly to his feet, blinking a little.

He never left the cinema very quickly. It always took him a moment or two to return to the prosaic reality of everyday life.

He glanced round. Not many people this afternoon – naturally. They were all at the races. Mr Leadbetter did not approve of racing nor of playing cards nor of drinking nor of smoking. This left him more energy to enjoy going to the pictures.

Everyone was hurrying towards the exit. Mr Leadbetter prepared to follow suit. The man in the seat in front of him was asleep – slumped down in his chair. Mr

Leadbetter felt indignant to think that anyone could sleep with such a drama as *Not a Sparrow* going on.

An irate gentleman was saying to the sleeping man whose legs were stretched out blocking the way:

'Excuse *me*, sir.'

Mr Leadbetter reached the exit. He looked back.

There seemed to be some sort of commotion. A commissionaire . . . a little knot of people . . . Perhaps that man in front of him was dead drunk and not asleep . . .

He hesitated and then passed out – and in so doing missed the sensation of the day – a greater sensation even than Not Half winning the St Leger at 85 to 1.

The commissionaire was saying:

'Believe you're right, sir . . . He's ill . . . Why – what's the matter, sir?'

The other had drawn away his hand with an exclamation and was examining a red sticky smear.

'Blood . . .'

The commissionaire gave a stifled exclamation.

He had caught sight of the corner of something yellow projecting from under the seat.

'Gor blimey!' he said. '*It's a b – A B C.*'

Chapter 25

Not from Captain Hastings' Personal Narrative

Mr Cust came out of the Regal Cinema and looked up at the sky.

A beautiful evening . . . A really beautiful evening . . .

A quotation from Browning came into his head.

'God's in His heaven. All's right with the world.'

He had always been fond of that quotation.

Only there were times, very often, when he had felt it wasn't true . . .

He trotted along the street smiling to himself until he came to the Black Swan where he was staying.

He climbed the stairs to his bedroom, a stuffy little room on the second floor, giving over a paved inner court and garage.

As he entered the room his smile faded suddenly. There was a stain on his sleeve near the cuff. He touched it tentatively – wet and red – blood . . .

His hand dipped into his pocket and brought out something – a long slender knife. The blade of that, too, was sticky and red . . .

Mr Cust sat there a long time.

Once his eyes shot round the room like those of a hunted animal.

His tongue passed feverishly over his lips . . .

'It isn't my fault,' said Mr Cust.

He sounded as though he were arguing with somebody – a schoolboy pleading to his headmaster.

He passed his tongue over his lips again . . .

Again, tentatively, he felt his coat sleeve.

His eyes crossed the room to the wash-basin.

A minute later he was pouring out water from the old-fashioned jug into the basin. Removing his coat, he rinsed the sleeve, carefully squeezing it out . . .

Ugh! The water was red now . . .

A tap on the door.

He stood there frozen into immobility – staring.

The door opened. A plump young woman – jug in hand.

'Oh, excuse me, sir. Your hot water, sir.'

He managed to speak then.

'Thank you . . . I've washed in cold . . .'

Why had he said that? Immediately her eyes went to the basin.

He said frenziedly: 'I – I've cut my hand . . .'

There was a pause – yes, surely a very long pause – before she said: 'Yes, sir.'

She went out, shutting the door.

Mr Cust stood as though turned to stone.

He listened.

It had come – at last . . .

Were there voices – exclamations – feet mounting the stairs?

He could hear nothing but the beating of his own heart . . .

Then, suddenly, from frozen immobility he leaped into activity.

He slipped on his coat, tiptoed to the door and opened it. No noises as yet except the familiar murmur arising from the bar. He crept down the stairs . . .

Still no one. That was luck. He paused at the foot of the stairs. Which way now?

He made up his mind, darted quickly along a passage and out by the door that gave into the yard. A couple of chauffeurs were there tinkering with cars and discussing winners and losers.

Mr Cust hurried across the yard and out into the street.

Round the first corner to the right – then to the left – right again . . .

Dare he risk the station?

Yes – there would be crowds there – special trains –

if luck were on his side he would do it all right . . .

If only luck were with him . . .

Chapter 26

Not from Captain Hastings' Personal Narrative

Inspector Crome was listening to the excited utterances of Mr Leadbetter.

'I assure you, inspector, my heart misses a beat when I think of it. He must actually have been sitting beside me all through the programme!'

Inspector Crome, completely indifferent to the behaviour of Mr Leadbetter's heart, said:

'Just let me have it quite clear? This man went out towards the close of the big picture –'

'*Not a Sparrow* – Katherine Royal,' murmured Mr Leadbetter automatically.

'He passed you and in doing so stumbled –'

'He *pretended* to stumble, I see it now. Then he leaned over the seat in front to pick up his hat. He must have stabbed the poor fellow then.'

'You didn't hear anything? A cry? Or a groan?'

Mr Leadbetter had heard nothing but the loud, hoarse accents of Katherine Royal, but in the vividness of his imagination he invented a groan.

Inspector Crome took the groan at its face value and bade him proceed.

'And then he went out –'

'Can you describe him?'

'He was a very big man. Six foot at least. A giant.'

'Fair or dark?'

'I – well – I'm not exactly sure. I think he was bald. A sinister-looking fellow.'

'He didn't limp, did he?' asked Inspector Crome.

'Yes – yes, now you come to speak of it I think he did limp. Very dark, he might have been some kind of half-caste.'

'Was he in his seat the last time the lights came up?'

'No. He came in after the big picture began.'

Inspector Crome nodded, handed Mr Leadbetter a statement to sign and got rid of him.

'That's about as bad a witness as you'll find,' he remarked pessimistically. 'He'd say anything with a little leading. It's perfectly clear that he hasn't the faintest idea what our man looks like. Let's have the commissionaire back.'

The commissionaire, very stiff and military, came in and stood to attention, his eyes fixed on Colonel Anderson.

'Now, then, Jameson, let's hear your story.'

Jameson saluted.

'Yessir. Close of the performance, sir. I was told there was a gentleman taken ill, sir. Gentleman was in the two and fourpennies, slumped down in his seat like. Other gentlemen standing around. Gentleman looked bad to me, sir. One of the gentlemen standing by put his hand to the ill gentleman's coat and drew my attention. Blood, sir. It was clear the gentleman was dead – stabbed, sir. My attention was drawn to an A B C railway guide, sir, under the seat. Wishing to act correctly, I did not touch same, but reported to the police immediately that a tragedy had occurred.'

'Very good. Jameson, you acted very properly.'

'Thank you, sir.'

'Did you notice a man leaving the two and fourpennies about five minutes earlier?'

'There were several, sir.'

'Could you describe them?'

'Afraid not, sir. One was Mr Geoffrey Parnell. And there was a young fellow, Sam Baker, with his young lady. I didn't notice anybody else particular.'

'A pity. That'll do, Jameson.'

'Yessir.'

The commissionaire saluted and departed.

'The medical details we've got,' said Colonel Anderson. 'We'd better have the fellow that found him next.'

A police constable came in and saluted.

'Mr Hercule Poirot's here, sir, and another gentleman.'

Inspector Crome frowned.

'Oh, well,' he said. 'Better have 'em in, I suppose.'

Chapter 27

The Doncaster Murder

Coming in hard on Poirot's heels, I just caught the fag end of Inspector Crome's remark.

Both he and the Chief Constable were looking worried and depressed.

Colonel Anderson greeted us with a nod of the head.

'Glad you've come, M. Poirot,' he said politely. I think he guessed that Crome's remark might have reached our ears. 'We've got it in the neck again, you see.'

'Another A B C murder?'

'Yes. Damned audacious bit of work. Man leaned over and stabbed the fellow in the back.'

'Stabbed this time?'

'Yes, varies his methods a bit, doesn't he? Biff on the head, strangled, now a knife. Versatile devil – what? Here are the medical details if you care to see 'em.'

He shoved a paper towards Poirot. 'A B C down on the floor between the dead man's feet,' he added.

'Has the dead man been identified?' asked Poirot.

'Yes. A B C's slipped up for once – if that's any satisfaction to us. Deceased's a man called Earlsfield – George Earlsfield. Barber by profession.'

'Curious,' commented Poirot.

'May have skipped a letter,' suggested the colonel.

My friend shook his head doubtfully.

'Shall we have in the next witness?' asked Crome. 'He's anxious to get home.'

'Yes, yes – let's get on.'

A middle-aged gentleman strongly resembling the frog footman in *Alice in Wonderland* was led in. He was highly excited and his voice was shrill with emotion.

'Most shocking experience I have ever known,' he squeaked. 'I have a weak heart, sir – a very weak heart, it might have been the death of me.'

'Your name, please,' said the inspector.

'Downes. Roger Emmanuel Downes.'

'Profession?'

'I am a master at Highfield School for boys.'

'Now, Mr Downes, will you tell us in your own words what happened.'

'I can tell you that very shortly, gentlemen. At the close of the performance I rose from my seat. The seat on my left was empty but in the one beyond a man was sitting, apparently asleep. I was unable to pass him to get out as his legs were stuck out in front of him. I asked him to allow me to pass. As he did not move I repeated my request in – a – er – slightly louder tone. He still made no response. I then took him by the shoulder to waken him. His body slumped down further and I became aware that he was either unconscious or seriously ill. I called out: "This gentleman is taken ill. Fetch the commissionaire." The commissionaire came. As I took my hand from the man's shoulder I found it was wet and red . . . I can assure you, gentlemen, the shock was terrific! Anything might have happened! For years I have suffered from cardiac weakness –'

Colonel Anderson was looking at Mr Downes with a very curious expression.

'You can consider that you're a lucky man, Mr Downes.'

'I do, sir. Not even a palpitation!'

'You don't quite take my meaning, Mr Downes. You were sitting two seats away, you say?'

'Actually I was sitting at first in the next seat to the murdered man – then I moved along so as to be behind an empty seat.'

'You're about the same height and build as the dead man, aren't you, and you were wearing a woollen scarf round your neck just as he was?'

'I fail to see –' began Mr Downes stiffly.

'I'm telling you, man,' said Colonel Anderson, 'just where your luck came in. Somehow or other, when the murderer followed you in, he got confused. *He picked on the wrong back.* I'll eat my hat, Mr Downes, if that knife wasn't meant for you!'

However well Mr Downes' heart had stood former tests, it was unable to stand up to this one. He sank on a chair, gasped, and turned purple in the face.

'Water,' he gasped. 'Water . . .'

A glass was brought him. He sipped it whilst his complexion gradually returned to the normal.

'Me?' he said. 'Why me?'

'It looks like it,' said Crome. 'In fact, it's the only explanation.'

'You mean that this man – this – this fiend incarnate – this bloodthirsty madman has been following *me* about waiting for an opportunity?'

'I should say that was the way of it.'

'But in heaven's name, why *me*?' demanded the outraged schoolmaster.

Inspector Crome struggled with the temptation to reply: 'Why not?' and said instead: 'I'm afraid it's no good expecting a lunatic to have reasons for what he does.'

'God bless my soul,' said Mr Downes, sobered into whispering.

He got up. He looked suddenly old and shaken.

'If you don't want me any more, gentlemen, I think I'll go home. I – I don't feel very well.'

'That's quite all right, Mr Downes. I'll send a constable with you – just to see you're all right.'

'Oh, no – no, thank you. That's not necessary.'

'Might as well,' said Colonel Anderson gruffly.

His eyes slid sideways, asking an imperceptible question of the inspector. The latter gave an equally imperceptible nod.

Mr Downes went out shakily.

'Just as well he didn't tumble to it,' said Colonel Anderson. 'There'll be a couple of them – eh?'

'Yes, sir. Your Inspector Rice has made arrangements. The house will be watched.'

'You think,' said Poirot, 'that when A B C finds out his mistake he might try again?'

Anderson nodded.

'It's a possibility,' he said. 'Seems a methodical sort of chap, A B C. It will upset him if things don't go according to programme.'

Poirot nodded thoughtfully.

'Wish we could get a description of the fellow,' said Colonel Anderson irritably. 'We're as much in the dark as ever.'

'It may come,' said Poirot.

'Think so? Well, it's possible. Damn it all, hasn't anyone got eyes in their head?'

'Have patience,' said Poirot.

'You seem very confident, M. Poirot. Got any reason for this optimism?'

'Yes, Colonel Anderson. Up to now, the murderer has not made a mistake. He is bound to make one soon.'

'If that's all you've got to go on,' began the Chief Constable with a snort, but he was interrupted.

'Mr Ball of the Black Swan is here with a young woman, sir. He reckons he's got summat to say might help you.'

'Bring them along. Bring them along. We can do with anything helpful.'

Mr Ball of the Black Swan was a large, slow-thinking, heavily moving man. He exhaled a strong odour of beer. With him was a plump young woman with round eyes clearly in a state of high excitement.

'Hope I'm not intruding or wasting valuable time,' said Mr Ball in a slow, thick voice. 'But this wench, Mary here, reckons she's got something to tell as you ought to know.'

Mary giggled in a half-hearted way.

'Well, my girl, what is it?' said Anderson. 'What's your name?'

'Mary, sir, Mary Stroud.'

'Well, Mary, out with it.'

Mary turned her round eyes on her master.

'It's her business to take up hot water to the gents' bedrooms,' said Mr Ball, coming to the rescue. 'About half a dozen gentlemen we'd got staying. Some for the races and some just commercials.'

'Yes, yes,' said Anderson impatiently.

'Get on, lass,' said Mr Ball. 'Tell your tale. Nowt to be afraid of.'

Mary gasped, groaned and plunged in a breathless voice into her narrative.

'I knocked on door and there wasn't no answer, otherwise I wouldn't have gone in leastways not unless the gentleman had said "Come in," and as he didn't say nothing I went in and he was there washing his hands.'

She paused and breathed deeply.

'Go on, my girl,' said Anderson.

Mary looked sideways at her master and as though receiving inspiration from his slow nod, plunged on again.

'"It's your hot water, sir," I said, "and I did knock," but "Oh," he says, "I've washed in cold," he said, and so, naturally, I looks in basin, and oh! God help me, sir, *it were all red!*'

'Red?' said Anderson sharply.

Ball struck in.

'The lass told me that he had his coat off and that he was holding the sleeve of it, and it was all wet – that's right, eh, lass?'

'Yes, sir, that's right, sir.'

She plunged on:

'And his face, sir, it looked queer, mortal queer it looked. Gave me quite a turn.'

'When was this?' asked Anderson sharply.

'About a quarter after five, so near as I can reckon.'

'Over three hours ago,' snapped Anderson. 'Why didn't you come at once?'

'Didn't hear about it at once,' said Ball. 'Not till news came along as there'd been another murder done. And then the lass she screams out as it might have been blood in the basin, and I asks her what she means, and she tells me. Well, it doesn't sound right to me and I went upstairs myself. Nobody in the room. I asks a few questions and one of the lads in courtyard says he saw a fellow sneaking out that way and by his description it was the right one. So I says to the missus as Mary here had best go to police. She doesn't like the idea, Mary doesn't, and I says I'll come along with her.'

Inspector Crome drew a sheet of paper towards him.

'Describe this man,' he said. 'As quick as you can. There's no time to be lost.'

'Medium-sized he were,' said Mary. 'And stooped and wore glasses.'

'His clothes?'

'A dark suit and a Homburg hat. Rather shabby-looking.'

She could add little to this description.

Inspector Crome did not insist unduly. The telephone wires were soon busy, but neither the inspector nor the Chief Constable were over-optimistic.

Crome elicited the fact that the man, when seen sneaking across the yard, had had no bag or suitcase.

'There's a chance there,' he said.

Two men were despatched to the Black Swan.

Mr Ball, swelling with pride and importance, and Mary, somewhat tearful, accompanied them.

The sergeant returned about ten minutes later.

'I've brought the register, sir,' he said. 'Here's the signature.'

We crowded round. The writing was small and cramped – not easy to read.

'A. B. Case – or is it Cash?' said the Chief Constable.

'A B C,' said Crome significantly.

'What about luggage?' asked Anderson.

'One good-sized suitcase, sir, full of small cardboard boxes.'

'Boxes? What was in 'em?'

'Stockings, sir. Silk stockings.'

Crome turned to Poirot.

'Congratulations,' he said. 'Your hunch was right.'

Chapter 28

Not from Captain Hastings' Personal Narrative

Inspector Crome was in his office at Scotland Yard.

The telephone on his desk gave a discreet buzz and he picked it up.

'Jacobs speaking, sir. There's a young fellow come in with a story that I think you ought to hear.'

Inspector Crome sighed. On an average twenty people a day turned up with so-called important information about the A B C case. Some of them were harmless lunatics, some of them were well-meaning persons who genuinely believed that their information was of value. It was the duty of Sergeant Jacobs to act as a human sieve – retaining the grosser matter and passing on the residue to his superior.

'Very well, Jacobs,' said Crome. 'Send him along.'

A few minutes later there was a tap on the inspector's door and Sergeant Jacobs appeared, ushering in a tall, moderately good-looking young man.

'This is Mr Tom Hartigan, sir. He's got something to tell us which may have a possible bearing on the A B C case.'

The inspector rose pleasantly and shook hands.

'Good morning, Mr Hartigan. Sit down, won't you? Smoke? Have a cigarette?'

Tom Hartigan sat down awkwardly and looked with some awe at what he called in his own mind 'One of the big-wigs.' The appearance of the inspector vaguely disappointed him. He looked quite an ordinary person!

'Now then,' said Crome. 'You've got something to tell us that you think may have a bearing on the case. Fire ahead.'

Tom began nervously.

'Of course it may be nothing at all. It's just an idea of mine. I may be wasting your time.'

Again Inspector Crome sighed imperceptibly. The amount of time he had to waste in reassuring people!

'We're the best judge of that. Let's have the facts, Mr Hartigan.'

'Well, it's like this, sir. I've got a young lady, you see, and her mother lets rooms. Up Camden Town way. Their second-floor back has been let for over a year to a man called Cust.'

'Cust – eh?'

'That's right, sir. A sort of middle-aged bloke what's

rather vague and soft – and come down in the world a bit, I should say. Sort of creature who wouldn't hurt a fly you'd say – and I'd never of dreamed of anything being wrong if it hadn't been for something rather odd.'

In a somewhat confused manner and repeating himself once or twice, Tom described his encounter with Mr Cust at Euston Station and the incident of the dropped ticket.

'You see, sir, look at it how you will, it's funny like. Lily – that's my young lady, sir – she was quite positive that it was Cheltenham he said, and her mother says the same – says she remembers distinct talking about it the morning he went off. Of course, I didn't pay much attention to it at the time. Lily – my young lady – said as how she hoped he wouldn't cop it from this A B C fellow going to Doncaster – and then she says it's rather a coincidence because he was down Churston way at the time of the last crime. Laughing like, I asks her whether he was at Bexhill the time before, and she says she don't know where he was, but he was away at the seaside – that she does know. And then I said to her it would be odd if he was the A B C himself and she said poor Mr Cust wouldn't hurt a fly – and that was all at the time. We didn't think no more about it. At least, in a sort of way I did, sir, underneath like. I began wondering about this Cust fellow and thinking that, after all, harmless as he seemed, he might be a bit batty.'

Tom took a breath and then went on. Inspector Crome was listening intently now.

'And then after the Doncaster murder, sir, it was in all the papers that information was wanted as to the whereabouts of a certain A B Casê or Cash, and it gave a description that fitted well enough. First evening off I had, I went round to Lily's and asked her what her Mr Cust's initials were. She couldn't remember at first, but her mother did. Said they were A B right enough. Then we got down to it and tried to figure out if Cust had been away at the time of the first murder at Andover. Well, as you know, sir, it isn't too easy to remember things three months back. We had a job of it, but we got it fixed down in the end, because Mrs Marbury had a brother come from Canada to see her on June 21st. He arrived unexpected like and she wanted to give him a bed, and Lily suggested that as Mr Cust was away Bert Smith might have his bed. But Mrs Marbury wouldn't agree, because she said it wasn't acting right by her lodger, and she always liked to act fair and square. But we fixed the date all right because of Bert Smith's ship docking at Southampton that day.'

Inspector Crome had listened very attentively, jotting down an occasional note.

'That's all?' he asked.

'That's all, sir. I hope you don't think I'm making a lot of nothing.'

Tom flushed slightly.

'Not at all. You were quite right to come here. Of course, it's very slight evidence – these dates may be mere coincidence and the likeness of the name, too. But it certainly warrants my having an interview with your Mr Cust. Is he at home now?'

'Yes, sir.'

'When did he return?'

'The evening of the Doncaster murder, sir.'

'What's he been doing since?'

'He's stayed in mostly, sir. And he's been looking very queer, Mrs Marbury says. He buys a lot of newspapers – goes out early and gets the morning ones, and then after dark he goes out and gets the evening ones. Mrs Marbury says he talks a lot to himself, too. She thinks he's getting queerer.'

'What is this Mrs Marbury's address?'

Tom gave it to him.

'Thank you. I shall probably be calling round in the course of the day. I need hardly tell you to be careful of your manner if you come across this Cust.'

He rose and shook hands.

'You may be quite satisfied you did the right thing in coming to us. Good morning, Mr Hartigan.'

'Well, sir?' asked Jacobs, re-entering the room a few

minutes later. 'Think it's the goods?'

'It's promising,' said Inspector Crome. 'That is, if the facts are as the boy stated them. We've had no luck with the stocking manufacturers yet. It was time we got hold of something. By the way, give me that file of the Churston case.'

He spent some minutes looking for what he wanted.

'Ah, here it is. It's amongst the statements made to the Torquay police. Young man of the name of Hill. Deposes he was leaving the Torquay Palladium after the film *Not a Sparrow* and noticed a man behaving queerly. He was talking to himself. Hill heard him say "That's an idea." *Not a Sparrow* – that's the film that was on at the Regal in Doncaster?'

'Yes, sir.'

'There may be something in that. Nothing to it at the time – but it's possible that the idea of the *modus operandi* for his next crime occurred to our man then. We've got Hill's name and address, I see. His description of the man is vague but it links up well enough with the descriptions of Mary Stroud and this Tom Hartigan . . .'

He nodded thoughtfully.

'We're getting warm,' said Inspector Crome – rather inaccurately, for he himself was always slightly chilly.

'Any instructions, sir?'

'Put on a couple of men to watch this Camden Town

address, but I don't want our bird frightened. I must have a word with the AC. Then I think it would be as well if Cust was brought along here and asked if he'd like to make a statement. It sounds as though he's quite ready to get rattled.'

Outside Tom Hartigan had rejoined Lily Marbury who was waiting for him on the Embankment.

'All right, Tom?'

Tom nodded.

'I saw Inspector Crome himself. The one who's in charge of the case.'

'What's he like?'

'A bit quiet and lah-di-dah – not my idea of a detective.'

'That's Lord Trenchard's new kind,' said Lily with respect. 'Some of them are ever so grand. Well, what did he say?'

Tom gave her a brief résumé of the interview.

'So they think as it really was him?'

'They think it might be. Anyway, they'll come along and ask him a question or two.'

'Poor Mr Cust.'

'It's no good saying poor Mr Cust, my girl. If he's A B C, he's committed four terrible murders.'

Lily sighed and shook her head.

'It does seem awful,' she observed.

'Well, now you're going to come and have a bite of

lunch, my girl. Just you think that if we're right I expect my name will be in the papers!'

'Oh, Tom, will it?'

'Rather. And yours, too. *And* your mother's. And I dare say you'll have your picture in it, too.'

'Oh, Tom.' Lily squeezed his arm in an ecstasy.

'And in the meantime what do you say to a bite at the Corner House?'

Lily squeezed tighter.

'Come on then!'

'All right – half a minute. I must just telephone from the station.'

'Who to?'

'A girl I was going to meet.'

She slipped across the road, and rejoined him three minutes later, looking rather flushed.

'Now then, Tom.'

She slipped her arm in his.

'Tell me more about Scotland Yard. You didn't see the other one there?'

'What other one?'

'The Belgian gentleman. The one that A B C writes to always.'

'No. He wasn't there.'

'Well, tell me all about it. What happened when you got inside? Who did you speak to and what did you say?'

II

Mr Cust put the receiver back very gently on the hook.

He turned to where Mrs Marbury was standing in the doorway of the room, clearly devoured with curiosity.

'Not often you have a telephone call, Mr Cust?'

'No – er – no, Mrs Marbury. It isn't.'

'Not bad news, I trust?'

'No – no.' How persistent the woman was. His eyes caught the legend on the newspaper he was carrying.

Births – Marriages – Deaths . . .

'My sister's just had a little boy,' he blurted out.

He – who had never had a sister!

'Oh, dear! Now – well, that *is* nice, I am sure. ("And never once mentioned a sister all these years," was her inward thought. "If that isn't just like a man!") I was surprised, I'll tell you, when the lady asked to speak to Mr Cust. Just at first I fancied it was my Lily's voice – something like hers, it was – but haughtier if you know what I mean – sort of high up in the air. Well, Mr Cust, my congratulations, I'm sure. Is it the first one, or have you other little nephews and nieces?'

'It's the only one,' said Mr Cust. 'The only one I've ever had or likely to have, and – er – I think I must go off at once. They – they want me to come. I – I think I can just catch a train if I hurry.'

'Will you be away long, Mr Cust?' called Mrs Marbury as he ran up the stairs.

'Oh, no – two or three days – that's all.'

He disappeared into his bedroom. Mrs Marbury retired into the kitchen, thinking sentimentally of 'the dear little mite'.

Her conscience gave her a sudden twinge.

Last night Tom and Lily and all the hunting back over dates! Trying to make out that Mr Cust was that dreadful monster, A B C. Just because of his initials and because of a few coincidences.

'I don't suppose they meant it seriously,' she thought comfortably. 'And now I hope they'll be ashamed of themselves.'

In some obscure way that she could not have explained, Mr Cust's statement that his sister had had a baby had effectually removed any doubts Mrs Marbury might have had of her lodger's *bona fides*.

'I hope she didn't have too hard a time of it, poor dear,' thought Mrs Marbury, testing an iron against her cheek before beginning to iron out Lily's silk slip.

Her mind ran comfortably on a well-worn obstetric track.

Mr Cust came quietly down the stairs, a bag in his hand. His eyes rested a minute on the telephone.

That brief conversation re-echoed in his brain.

'Is that you, Mr Cust? I thought you might like to know there's an inspector from Scotland Yard may be coming to see you . . .'

What had he said? He couldn't remember.

'Thank you – thank you, my dear . . . very kind of you . . .'

Something like that.

Why had she telephoned to him? Could she possibly have guessed? Or did she just want to make sure he would stay in for the inspector's visit?

But how did she know the inspector was coming?

And her voice – she'd disguised her voice from her mother . . .

It looked – it looked – as though she *knew* . . .

But surely if she knew, she wouldn't . . .

She might, though. Women were very queer. Unexpectedly cruel and unexpectedly kind. He'd seen Lily once letting a mouse out of a mouse-trap.

A kind girl . . .

A kind, pretty girl . . .

He paused by the hall stand with its load of umbrellas and coats.

Should he . . . ?

A slight noise from the kitchen decided him . . .

No, there wasn't time . . .

Mrs Marbury might come out . . .

He opened the front door, passed through and closed it behind him . . .

Where . . . ?

Chapter 29

At Scotland Yard

Conference again.

The Assistant Commissioner, Inspector Crome, Poirot and myself.

The AC was saying:

'A good tip that of yours, M. Poirot, about checking a large sale of stockings.'

Poirot spread out his hands.

'It was indicated. This man could not be a regular agent. He sold outright instead of touting for orders.'

'Got everything clear so far, inspector?'

'I think so, sir.' Crome consulted a file. 'Shall I run over the position to date?'

'Yes, please.'

'I've checked up with Churston, Paignton and Torquay. Got a list of people where he went and offered stockings. I must say he did the thing thoroughly. Stayed at the Pitt, small hotel near Torre Station. Returned to the hotel at 10.30 on the night of the murder. Could have taken a train from Churston at 9.57, getting to Torre at 10.20. No one answering to his description noticed on train or at station, but that Friday was Dartmouth Regatta and the trains back from Kingswear were pretty full.

'Bexhill much the same. Stayed at the Globe under his own name. Offered stockings to about a dozen addresses, including Mrs Barnard and including the Ginger Cat. Left hotel early in the evening. Arrived back in London about 11.30 the following morning. As to Andover, same procedure. Stayed at the Feathers. Offered stockings to Mrs Fowler, next door to Mrs Ascher, and to half a dozen other people in the street. The pair Mrs Ascher had I got from the niece (name of Drower) – they're identical with Cust's supply.'

'So far, good,' said the AC.

'Acting on information received,' said the inspector, 'I went to the address given me by Hartigan, but found that Cust had left the house about half an hour previously. He received a telephone message, I'm told. First time such a thing had happened to him, so his landlady told me.'

'An accomplice?' suggested the Assistant Commissioner.

'Hardly,' said Poirot. 'It is odd that – unless –'

We all looked at him inquiringly as he paused.

He shook his head, however, and the inspector proceeded.

'I made a thorough search of the room he had occupied. That search puts the matter beyond doubt. I found a block of notepaper similar to that on which the letters were written, a large quantity of hosiery and – at the back of the cupboard where the hosiery was stored – a parcel much the same shape and size but which turned out to contain – not hosiery – *but eight new A B C railway guides!*'

'Proof positive,' said the Assistant Commissioner.

'I've found something else, too,' said the inspector – his voice becoming suddenly almost human with triumph. 'Only found it this morning, sir. Not had time to report yet. There was no sign of the knife in his room –'

'It would be the act of an imbecile to bring that back with him,' remarked Poirot.

'After all, he's not a reasonable human being,' remarked the inspector. 'Anway, it occurred to me that he might just possibly have brought it back to the house and then realized the danger of hiding it (as M. Poirot points out) in his room, and have looked about elsewhere. What place in the house would he be likely to select? I got it straight away. *The hall stand* – no one ever moves a hall stand. With a lot of trouble I got it moved out from the wall – and there it was!'

'The knife?'

'The knife. Not a doubt of it. The dried blood's still on it.'

'Good work, Crome,' said the AC approvingly. 'We only need one thing more now.'

'What's that?'

'The man himself.'

'We'll get him, sir. Never fear.'

The inspector's tone was confident.

'What do you say, M. Poirot?'

Poirot started out of a reverie.

'I beg your pardon?'

'We were saying that it was only a matter of time before we got our man. Do you agree?'

'Oh, that – yes. Without a doubt.'

His tone was so abstracted that the others looked at him curiously.

'Is there anything worrying you, M. Poirot?'

'There is something that worries me very much. It is the *why*? The *motive*.'

'But, my dear fellow, the man's crazy,' said the Assistant Commissioner impatiently.

'I understand what M. Poirot means,' said Crome, coming graciously to the rescue. 'He's quite right. There's got to be some definite obsession. I think we'll find the root of the matter in an intensified inferiority complex. There may be a persecution mania, too, and if so he may possibly associate M. Poirot with it. He may have the delusion that M. Poirot is a detective employed on purpose to hunt him down.'

'H'm,' said the AC. 'That's the jargon that's talked nowadays. In my day if a man was mad he was mad and we didn't look about for scientific terms to soften it down. I suppose a thoroughly up-to-date doctor would suggest putting a man like A B C in a nursing home, telling him what a fine fellow he was for forty-five days on end and then letting him out as a responsible member of society.'

Poirot smiled but did not answer.

The conference broke up.

'Well,' said the Assistant Commissioner. 'As you say, Crome, pulling him in is only a matter of time.'

'We'd have had him before now,' said the inspector, 'if he wasn't so ordinary-looking. We've worried enough perfectly inoffensive citizens as it is.'

'I wonder where he is at this minute,' said the Assistant Commissioner.

Chapter 30

Not from Captain Hastings' Personal Narrative

Mr Cust stood by a greengrocer's shop.

He stared across the road.

Yes, that was it.

Mrs Ascher. Newsagent and Tobacconist . . .

In the empty window was a sign.

To Let.

Empty . . .

Lifeless . . .

'Excuse me, sir.'

The greengrocer's wife, trying to get at some lemons.

He apologized, moved to one side.

Slowly he shuffled away – back towards the main street of the town . . .

It was difficult – very difficult – now that he hadn't any money left . . .

Not having had anything to eat all day made one feel very queer and light-headed . . .

He looked at a poster outside a newsagent's shop.

The A B C Case. Murderer Still at Large. Interviews with M. Hercule Poirot.

Mr Cust said to himself:

'Hercule Poirot. I wonder if *he* knows . . .'

He walked on again.

It wouldn't do to stand staring at that poster . . .

He thought:

'I can't go on much longer . . .'

Foot in front of foot . . . what an odd thing walking was . . .

Foot in front of foot – ridiculous.

Highly ridiculous . . .

But man was a ridiculous animal anyway . . .

And he, Alexander Bonaparte Cust, was particularly ridiculous.

He had always been . . .

People had always laughed at him . . .

He couldn't blame them . . .

Where was he going? He didn't know. He'd come to the end. He no longer looked anywhere but at his feet.

Foot in front of foot.

He looked up. Lights in front of him. And letters . . .

Police Station.

'That's funny,' said Mr Cust. He gave a little giggle.

Then he stepped inside. Suddenly, as he did so, he swayed and fell forward.

Chapter 31

Hercule Poirot Asks Questions

It was a clear November day. Dr Thompson and Chief Inspector Japp had come round to acquaint Poirot with the result of the police court proceedings in the case of Rex *v.* Alexander Bonaparte Cust.

Poirot himself had had a slight bronchial chill which had prevented his attending. Fortunately he had not insisted on having my company.

'Committed for trial,' said Japp. 'So that's that.'

'Isn't it unusual?' I asked, 'for a defence to be offered at this stage? I thought prisoners always reserved their defence.'

'It's the usual course,' said Japp. 'I suppose young Lucas thought he might rush it through. He's a trier, I will say. Insanity's the only defence possible.'

Poirot shrugged his shoulders.

'With insanity there can be no acquittal. Imprisonment during His Majesty's pleasure is hardly preferable to death.'

'I suppose Lucas thought there was a chance,' said Japp. 'With a first-class alibi for the Bexhill murder, the whole case might be weakened. I don't think he realized how strong our case is. Anyway, Lucas goes in for originality. He's a young man, and he wants to hit the public eye.'

Poirot turned to Thompson.

'What's your opinion, doctor?'

'Of Cust? Upon my soul, I don't know what to say. He's playing the sane man remarkably well. He's an epileptic, of course.'

'What an amazing dénouement that was,' I said.

'His falling into the Andover police station in a fit? Yes – it was a fitting dramatic curtain to the drama. A B C has always timed his effects well.'

'Is it possible to commit a crime and be unaware of it?' I asked. 'His denials seem to have a ring of truth in them.'

Dr Thompson smiled a little.

'You mustn't be taken in by that theatrical "I swear by God" pose. It's my opinion *that Cust knows perfectly well he committed the murders*.'

'When they're as fervent as that they usually do,' said Crome.

'As to your question,' went on Thompson, 'it's perfectly possible for an epileptic subject in a state of somnambulism to commit an action and be entirely unaware of having done so. But it is the general opinion that such an action must "not be contrary to the will of the person in the waking state".'

He went on discussing the matter, speaking of *grand mal* and *petit mal* and, to tell the truth, confusing me hopelessly as is often the case when a learned person holds forth on his own subject.

'However, I'm against the theory that Cust committed these crimes without knowing he'd done them. You might put that theory forward if it weren't for the letters. The letters knock the theory on the head. They show premeditation and a careful planning of the crime.'

'And of the letters we have still no explanation,' said Poirot.

'That interests you?'

'Naturally – since they were written to me. And on the subject of the letters Cust is persistently dumb. Until I get at the reason for those letters being written to me, I shall not feel that the case is solved.'

'Yes – I can understand that from your point of view. There doesn't seem to be any reason to believe that the man ever came up against you in any way?'

'None whatever.'

'I might make a suggestion. Your name!'

'My name?'

'Yes. Cust is saddled – apparently by the whim of his mother (Oedipus complex there, I shouldn't wonder!) – with two extremely bombastic Christian names: Alexander and Bonaparte. You see the implications? Alexander – the popularly supposed undefeatable who sighed for more worlds to conquer. Bonaparte – the great Emperor of the French. He wants an adversary – an adversary, one might say, in his class. Well – there you are – Hercules the strong.'

'Your words are very suggestive, doctor. They foster ideas . . .'

'Oh, it's only a suggestion. Well, I must be off.'

Dr Thompson went out. Japp remained.

'Does this alibi worry you?' Poirot asked.

'It does a little,' admitted the inspector. 'Mind you, I don't believe in it, because I know it isn't true. But it is going to be the deuce to break it. This man Strange is a tough character.'

'Describe him to me.'

'He's a man of forty. A tough, confident, self-opinionated mining engineer. It's my opinion that it was he who insisted on his evidence being taken now. He wants to get off to Chile. He hoped the thing might be settled out of hand.'

'He's one of the most positive people I've ever seen,' I said.

'The type of man who would not like to admit he was mistaken,' said Poirot thoughtfully.

'He sticks to his story and he's not one to be heckled.

He swears by all that's blue that he picked up Cust in the Whitecross Hotel at Eastbourne on the evening of July 24th. He was lonely and wanted someone to talk to. As far as I can see, Cust made an ideal listener. He didn't interrupt! After dinner he and Cust played dominoes. It appears Strange was a whale on dominoes and to his surprise Cust was pretty hot stuff too. Queer game, dominoes. People go mad about it. They'll play for hours. That's what Strange and Cust did apparently. Cust wanted to go to bed but Strange wouldn't hear of it – swore they'd keep it up until midnight at least. And that's what they did do. They separated at ten minutes past midnight. And if Cust was in the Whitecross Hotel at Eastbourne at ten minutes past midnight on the morning of the 25th he couldn't very well be strangling Betty Barnard on the beach at Bexhill between midnight and one o'clock.'

'The problem certainly seems insuperable,' said Poirot thoughtfully. 'Decidedly, it gives one to think.'

'It's given Crome something to think about,' said Japp.

'This man Strange is very positive?'

'Yes. He's an obstinate devil. And it's difficult to see just where the flaw is. Supposing Strange is making a mistake and the man wasn't Cust – why on earth should he *say* his name is Cust? And the writing in the hotel register is his all right. You can't say he's an accomplice

– homicidal lunatics don't have accomplices! Did the girl die later? The doctor was quite firm in his evidence, and anyway it would take some time for Cust to get out of the hotel at Eastbourne without being seen and get over to Bexhill – about fourteen miles away –'

'It is a problem – yes,' said Poirot.

'Of course, strictly speaking, it oughtn't to matter. We've got Cust on the Doncaster murder – the blood-stained coat, the knife – not a loophole there. You couldn't bounce any jury into acquitting him. But it spoils a pretty case. He did the Doncaster murder. He did the Churston murder. He did the Andover murder. Then, by hell, he *must* have done the Bexhill murder. But I don't see how!'

He shook his head and got up.

'Now's your chance, M. Poirot,' he said. 'Crome's in a fog. Exert those cellular arrangements of yours I used to hear so much about. Show us the way he did it.'

Japp departed.

'What about it, Poirot?' I said. 'Are the little grey cells equal to the task?'

Poirot answered my question by another.

'Tell me, Hastings, do you consider the case ended?'

'Well – yes, practically speaking. We've got the man. And we've got most of the evidence. It's only the trimmings that are needed.'

Poirot shook his head.

'The case is ended! The case! The case is the *man*, Hastings. Until we know all about the man, the mystery is as deep as ever. It is not victory because we have put him in the dock!'

'We know a fair amount about him.'

'We know nothing at all! We know where he was born. We know he fought in the war and received a slight wound in the head and that he was discharged from the army owing to epilepsy. We know that he lodged with Mrs Marbury for nearly two years. We know that he was quiet and retiring – the sort of man that nobody notices. We know that he invented and carried out an intensely clever scheme of systemized murder. We know that he made certain incredibly stupid blunders. We know that he killed without pity and quite ruthlessly. We know, too, that he was kindly enough not to let blame rest on any other person for the crimes he committed. If he wanted to kill unmolested – how easy to let other persons suffer for his crimes. Do you not see, Hastings, that the man is a mass of contradictions? Stupid and cunning, ruthless and magnanimous – *and that there must be some dominating factor that reconciles his two natures*.'

'Of course, if you treat him like a psychological study,' I began.

'What else has this case been since the beginning? All along I have been groping my way – trying *to get to know the murderer*. And now I realize, Hastings, *that I do not know him at all!* I am at sea.'

'The lust for power –' I began.

'Yes – that might explain a good deal . . . But it does not satisfy me. There are things I want to know. *Why* did he commit these murders? *Why* did he choose those particular people –?'

'Alphabetically –' I began.

'Was Betty Barnard the only person in Bexhill whose name began with a B? Betty Barnard – I had an idea there . . . It ought to be true – it must be true. But if so –'

He was silent for some time. I did not like to interrupt him.

As a matter of fact, I believe I fell asleep.

I woke to find Poirot's hand on my shoulder.

'*Mon cher Hastings*,' he said affectionately. 'My good genius.'

I was quite confused by this sudden mark of esteem.

'It is true,' Poirot insisted. 'Always – always – you help me – you bring me luck. You inspire me.'

'How have I inspired you this time?' I asked.

'While I was asking myself certain questions I remembered a remark of yours – a remark absolutely shimmering in its clear vision. Did I not say to you once that you had a genius for stating the obvious. It is the obvious that I have neglected.'

'What is this brilliant remark of mine?' I asked.

'It makes everything as clear as crystal. I see the answers to all my questions. The reason for Mrs Ascher (that, it is true, I glimpsed long ago), the reason for Sir Carmichael Clarke, the reason for the Doncaster murder, and finally and supremely important, *the reason for Hercule Poirot.*'

'Could you kindly explain?' I asked.

'Not at the moment. I require first a little more information. That I can get from our Special Legion. And then – then, *when I have got the answer to a certain question, I will go and see ABC.* We will be face to face at last – A B C and Hercule Poirot – the adversaries.'

'And then?' I asked.

'And then,' said Poirot. 'We will talk! *Je vous assure, Hastings* – there is nothing so dangerous *for anyone who has something to hide* as conversation! Speech, so a wise old Frenchman said to me once, is an invention of man's to prevent him from thinking. It is also an infallible means of discovering that which he wishes to hide. A human being, Hastings, cannot resist the opportunity to reveal himself and express his personality which conversation gives him. Every time he will give himself away.'

'What do you expect Cust to tell you?'

Hercule Poirot smiled.

'A lie,' he said. 'And by it, I shall know the truth!'

Chapter 32

And Catch a Fox

During the next few days Poirot was very busy. He made mysterious absences, talked very little, frowned to himself, and consistently refused to satisfy my natural curiosity as to the brilliance I had, according to him, displayed in the past.

I was not invited to accompany him on his mysterious comings and goings – a fact which I somewhat resented.

Towards the end of the week, however, he announced his intention of paying a visit to Bexhill and neighbourhood and suggested that I should come with him. Needless to say, I accepted with alacrity.

The invitation, I discovered, was not extended to me alone. The members of our Special Legion were also invited.

They were as intrigued by Poirot as I was. Nevertheless, by the end of the day, I had at any rate an idea as to the direction in which Poirot's thoughts were tending.

He first visited Mr and Mrs Barnard and got an exact account from her as to the hour at which Mr Cust had called on her and exactly what he had said. He then went to the hotel at which Cust had put up and extracted a minute description of that gentleman's departure. As far as I could judge, no new facts were elicited by his questions but he himself seemed quite satisfied.

Next he went to the beach – to the place where Betty Barnard's body had been discovered. Here he walked round in circles for some minutes studying the shingle attentively. I could see little point in this, since the tide covered the spot twice a day.

However I have learnt by this time that Poirot's actions are usually dictated by an idea – however meaningless they may seem.

He then walked from the beach to the nearest point at which a car could have been parked. From there again he went to the place where the Eastbourne buses waited before leaving Bexhill.

Finally he took us all to the Ginger Cat café, where we had a somewhat stale tea served by the plump waitress, Milly Higley.

Her he complimented in a flowing Gallic style on the shape of her ankles.

'The legs of the English – always they are too thin!

But you, mademoiselle, have the perfect leg. It has shape – it has an ankle!'

Milly Higley giggled a good deal and told him not to go on so. She knew what French gentlemen were like.

Poirot did not trouble to contradict her mistake as to his nationality. He merely ogled her in such a way that I was startled and almost shocked.

'*Voilà*,' said Poirot, 'I have finished in Bexhill. Presently I go to Eastbourne. One little inquiry there – that is all. Unnecessary for you all to accompany me. In the meantime come back to the hotel and let us have a cocktail. That Carlton tea, it was abominable!'

As we were sipping our cocktails Franklin Clarke said curiously:

'I suppose we can guess what you are after? You're out to break that alibi. But I can't see what you're so pleased about. You haven't got a new fact of any kind.'

'No – that is true.'

'Well, then?'

'Patience. Everything arranges itself, given time.'

'You seem quite pleased with yourself anyway.'

'Nothing so far has contradicted my little idea – that is why.'

His face grew serious.

'My friend Hastings told me once that he had, as a young man, played a game called The Truth. It was a game where everyone in turn was asked three questions

– two of which must be answered truthfully. The third one could be barred. The questions, naturally, were of the most indiscreet kind. But to begin with everyone had to swear that they would indeed speak the truth, and nothing but the truth.'

He paused.

'Well?' said Megan.

'*Eh bien* – me, I want to play that game. Only it is not necessary to have three questions. One will be enough. One question to each of you.'

'Of course,' said Clarke impatiently. 'We'll answer anything.'

'Ah, but I want it to be more serious than that. Do you all swear to speak the truth?'

He was so solemn about it that the others, puzzled, became solemn themselves. They all swore as he demanded.

'*Bon*,' said Poirot briskly. 'Let us begin –'

'I'm ready,' said Thora Grey.

'Ah, but ladies first – this time it would not be the politeness. We will start elsewhere.'

He turned to Franklin Clarke.

'What, *mon cher M. Clarke*, did you think of the hats the ladies wore at Ascot this year?'

Franklin Clarke stared at him.

'Is this a joke?'

'Certainly not.'

'Is that seriously your question?'

'It is.'

Clarke began to grin.

'Well, M. Poirot, I didn't actually go to Ascot, but from what I could see of them driving in cars, women's hats for Ascot were an even bigger joke than the hats they wear ordinarily.'

'Fantastic?'

'Quite fantastic.'

Poirot smiled and turned to Donald Fraser.

'When did you take your holiday this year, monsieur?'

It was Fraser's turn to stare.

'My holiday? The first two weeks in August.'

His face quivered suddenly. I guessed that the question had brought the loss of the girl he loved back to him.

Poirot, however, did not seem to pay much attention to the reply. He turned to Thora Grey and I heard the slight difference in his voice. It had tightened up. His question came sharp and clear.

'Mademoiselle, in the event of Lady Clarke's death, would you have married Sir Carmichael if he had asked you?'

The girl sprang up.

'How dare you ask me such a question. It's – it's insulting!'

'Perhaps. But you have sworn to speak the truth. *Eh bien* – Yes or no?'

'Sir Carmichael was wonderfully kind to me. He treated me almost like a daughter. And that's how I felt to him – just affectionate and grateful.'

'Pardon me, but that is not answering Yes or No, mademoiselle.'

She hesitated.

'The answer, of course, is no!'

He made no comment.

'Thank you, mademoiselle.'

He turned to Megan Barnard. The girl's face was very pale. She was breathing hard as though braced up for an ordeal.

Poirot's voice came out like the crack of a whiplash.

'Mademoiselle, what do you hope will be the result of my investigations? Do you want me to find out the truth – or not?'

Her head went back proudly. I was fairly sure of her answer. Megan, I knew, had a fanatical passion for truth.

Her answer came clearly – and it stupefied me.

'No!'

We all jumped. Poirot leant forward studying her face.

'Mademoiselle Megan,' he said, 'you may not want the truth but – *ma foi* – you can speak it!'

He turned towards the door, then, recollecting, went to Mary Drower.

'Tell me, *mon enfant*, have you a young man?'

Mary, who had been looking apprehensive, looked startled and blushed.

'Oh, Mr Poirot. I – I – well, I'm not sure.'

He smiled.

'*Alors c'est bien, mon enfant.*'

He looked round for me.

'Come, Hastings, we must start for Eastbourne.'

The car was waiting and soon we were driving along the coast road that leads through Pevensey to Eastbourne.

'Is it any use asking you anything, Poirot?'

'Not at this moment. Draw your own conclusions as to what I am doing.'

I relapsed into silence.

Poirot, who seemed pleased with himself, hummed a little tune. As we passed through Pevensey he suggested that we stop and have a look over the castle.

As we were returning towards the car, we paused a moment to watch a ring of children – Brownies, I guessed, by their get-up – who were singing a ditty in shrill, untuneful voices . . .

'What is it that they say, Hastings? I cannot catch the words.'

I listened – till I caught one refrain.

'– And catch a fox
And put him in a box
And never let him go.'

'And catch a fox and put him in a box and never let him go!' repeated Poirot.

His face had gone suddenly grave and stern.

'It is very terrible that, Hastings.' He was silent a minute. 'You hunt the fox here?'

'I don't. I've never been able to afford to hunt. And I don't think there's much hunting in this part of the world.'

'I meant in England generally. A strange sport. The waiting at the covert side – then they sound the tally-ho, do they not? – and the run begins – across the country – over the hedges and ditches – and the fox he runs – and sometimes he doubles back – but the dogs –'

'Hounds!'

'– hounds are on his trail, and at last they catch him and he dies – quickly and horribly.'

'I suppose it does sound cruel, but really –'

'The fox enjoys it? Do not say *les bêtises*, my friend. *Tout de même* – it is better that – the quick, cruel death – than what those children were singing . . .

'To be shut away – in a box – for ever . . . No, it is not good, that.'

He shook his head. Then he said, with a change of tone:

'Tomorrow, I am to visit the man Cust,' and he added to the chauffeur:

'Back to London.'

'Aren't you going to Eastbourne?' I cried.

'What need? I know – quite enough for my purpose.'

Chapter 33

Alexander Bonaparte Cust

I was not present at the interview that took place between Poirot and that strange man – Alexander Bonaparte Cust. Owing to his association with the police and the peculiar circumstances of the case, Poirot had no difficulty in obtaining a Home Office order – but that order did not extend to me, and in any case it was essential, from Poirot's point of view, that that interview should be absolutely private – the two men face to face.

He has given me, however, such a detailed account of what passed between them that I set it down with as much confidence on paper as though I had actually been present.

Mr Cust seemed to have shrunk. His stoop was more apparent. His fingers plucked vaguely at his coat.

For some time, I gather, Poirot did not speak.

He sat and looked at the man opposite him.

The atmosphere became restful – soothing – full of infinite leisure . . .

It must have been a dramatic moment – this meeting of the two adversaries in the long drama. In Poirot's place I should have felt the dramatic thrill.

Poirot, however, is nothing if not matter-of-fact. He was absorbed in producing a certain effect upon the man opposite him.

At last he said gently:

'Do you know who I am?'

The other shook his head.

'No – no – I can't say I do. Unless you are Mr Lucas's – what do they call it? – junior. Or perhaps you come from Mr Maynard?'

(Maynard & Cole were the defending solicitors.)

His tone was polite but not very interested. He seemed absorbed in some inner abstraction.

'I am Hercule Poirot . . .'

Poirot said the words very gently . . . and watched for the effect.

Mr Cust raised his head a little.

'Oh, yes?'

He said it as naturally as Inspector Crome might have said it – but without the superciliousness.

Then, a minute later, he repeated his remark.

'Oh, yes?' he said, and this time his tone was different

– it held an awakened interest. He raised his head and looked at Poirot.

Hercule Poirot met his gaze and nodded his own head gently once or twice.

'Yes,' he said. 'I am the man to whom you wrote the letters.'

At once the contact was broken. Mr Cust dropped his eyes and spoke irritably and fretfully.

'I never wrote to you. Those letters weren't written by me. I've said so again and again.'

'I know,' said Poirot. 'But if you did not write them, who did?'

'An enemy. I must have an enemy. They are all against me. The police – everyone – all against me. It's a gigantic conspiracy.'

Poirot did not reply.

Mr Cust said:

'Everyone's hand has been against me – always.'

'Even when you were a child?'

Mr Cust seemed to consider.

'No – no – not exactly then. My mother was very fond of me. But she was ambitious – terribly ambitious. That's why she gave me those ridiculous names. She had some absurd idea that I'd cut a figure in the world. She was always urging me to assert myself – talking about will-power . . . saying anyone could be master of his fate . . . she said I could do anything!'

He was silent for a minute.

'She was quite wrong, of course. I realized that myself quite soon. I wasn't the sort of person to get on in life. I was always doing foolish things – making myself look ridiculous. And I was timid – afraid of people. I had a bad time at school – the boys found out my Christian names – they used to tease me about them . . . I did very badly at school – in games and work and everything.'

He shook his head.

'Just as well poor mother died. She'd have been disappointed . . . Even when I was at the Commercial College I was stupid – it took me longer to learn typing and shorthand than anyone else. And yet I didn't *feel* stupid – if you know what I mean.'

He cast a sudden appealing look at the other man.

'I know what you mean,' said Poirot. 'Go on.'

'It was just the feeling that everybody else *thought* me stupid. Very paralysing. It was the same thing later in the office.'

'And later still in the war?' prompted Poirot.

Mr Cust's face lightened up suddenly.

'You know,' he said, 'I enjoyed the war. What I had of it, that was. I felt, for the first time, a man like anybody else. We were all in the same box. I was as good as anyone else.'

His smile faded.

'And then I got that wound on the head. Very slight.

But they found out I had fits . . . I'd always known, of course, that there were times when I hadn't been quite sure what I was doing. Lapses, you know. And of course, once or twice I'd fallen down. But I don't really think they ought to have discharged me for that. No, I don't think it was right.'

'And afterwards?' asked Poirot.

'I got a place as a clerk. Of course there was good money to be got just then. And I didn't do so badly after the war. Of course, a smaller salary . . . And – I didn't seem to get on. I was always being passed over for promotion. I wasn't go-ahead enough. It grew very difficult – really very difficult. . . . Especially when the slump came. To tell you the truth, I'd got hardly enough to keep body and soul together (and you've got to look presentable as a clerk) when I got the offer of this stocking job. A salary and commission!'

Poirot said gently:

'But you are aware, are you not, that the firm whom you say employed you deny the fact?'

Mr Cust got excited again.

'That's because they're in the conspiracy – they must be in the conspiracy.'

He went on:

'I've got written evidence – written evidence. I've got their letters to me, giving me instructions as to what places to go to and a list of people to call on.'

'Not *written* evidence exactly – *typewritten* evidence.'

'It's the same thing. Naturally a big firm of wholesale manufacturers typewrite their letters.'

'Don't you know, Mr Cust, that a typewriter can be identified? All those letters were typed by one particular machine.'

'What of it?'

'And that machine was your own – the one found in your room.'

'It was sent me by the firm at the beginning of my job.'

'Yes, but these letters were received *afterwards*. So it looks, does it not, as though *you typed them yourself and posted them to yourself?*'

'No, no! It's all part of the plot against me!'

He added suddenly:

'Besides, their letters *would* be written on the same kind of machine.'

'The same *kind*, but not the same actual machine.'

Mr Cust repeated obstinately:

'It's a plot!'

'And the A B C's that were found in the cupboard?'

'I know nothing about them. I thought they were all stockings.'

'Why did you tick off the name of Mrs Ascher in that first list of people in Andover?'

'Because I decided to start with her. One must begin somewhere.'

'Yes, that is true. *One must begin somewhere.*'

'I don't mean that!' said Mr Cust. 'I don't mean what you mean!'

'*But you know what I meant?*'

Mr Cust said nothing. He was trembling.

'I didn't do it!' he said. 'I'm perfectly innocent! It's all a mistake. Why, look at that second crime – that Bexhill one. I was playing dominoes at Eastbourne. You've got to admit that!'

His voice was triumphant.

'Yes,' said Poirot. His voice was meditative – silky. 'But it's so easy, isn't it, to make a mistake of one day? And if you're an obstinate, positive man, like Mr Strange, you'll never consider the possibility of having been mistaken. What you've said you'll stick to . . . He's that kind of man. And the hotel register – it's very easy to put down the wrong date when you're signing it – probably no one will notice it at the time.'

'I was playing dominoes that evening!'

'You play dominoes very well, I believe.'

Mr Cust was a little flurried by this.

'I – I – well, I believe I do.'

'It is a very absorbing game, is it not, with a lot of skill in it?'

'Oh, there's a lot of play in it – a lot of play! We used

to play a lot in the city, in the lunch hour. You'd be surprised the way total strangers come together over a game of dominoes.'

He chuckled.

'I remember one man – I've never forgotten him because of something he told me – we just got talking over a cup of coffee, and we started dominoes. Well, I felt after twenty minutes that I'd known that man all my life.'

'What was it that he told you?' asked Poirot.

Mr Cust's face clouded over.

'It gave me a turn – a nasty turn. Talking of your fate being written in your hand, he was. And he showed me his hand and the lines that showed he'd have two near escapes of being drowned – and he had had two near escapes. And then he looked at mine and he told me some amazing things. Said I was going to be one of the most celebrated men in England before I died. Said the whole country would be talking about me. But he said – he said . . .'

Mr Cust broke down – faltered . . .

'Yes?'

Poirot's gaze held a quiet magnetism. Mr Cust looked at him, looked away, then back again like a fascinated rabbit.

'He said – he said – that it looked as though I might die a violent death – and he laughed and said: "Almost looks as though you might die on the scaffold," and then he laughed and said that was only his joke . . .'

He was silent suddenly. His eyes left Poirot's face – they ran from side to side . . .

'My head – I suffer very badly with my head . . . the headaches are something cruel sometimes. And then there are times when I don't know – when I don't know . . .'

He broke down.

Poirot leant forward. He spoke very quietly but with great assurance.

'*But you do know, don't you,*' he said, '*that you committed the murders?*'

Mr Cust looked up. His glance was quite simple and direct. All resistance had left him. He looked strangely at peace.

'Yes,' he said, 'I know.'

'But – I am right, am I not? – *you don't know why you did them?*'

Mr Cust shook his head.

'No,' he said. 'I don't.'

Chapter 34

Poirot Explains

We were sitting in a state of tense attention to listen to Poirot's final explanation of the case.

'All along,' he said, 'I have been worried over the *why* of this case. Hastings said to me the other day that the case was ended. I replied to him that the case was the *man*! The mystery was *not the mystery of the murders*, but the *mystery of A B C*. Why did he find it necessary to commit these murders? Why did he select *me* as his adversary?

'It is no answer to say that the man was mentally unhinged. To say a man does mad things because he is mad is merely unintelligent and stupid. A madman is as logical and reasoned in his actions as a sane man – *given his peculiar biased point of view*. For example, if a man insists on going out and squatting about in nothing but a loin cloth his conduct seems eccentric in the extreme. But once you know *that the man himself is firmly convinced that he is Mahatma Gandhi*, then his conduct becomes perfectly reasonable and logical.

'What was necessary in this case was to imagine a mind so constituted *that it was logical and reasonable to commit four or more murders* and to announce them beforehand by letters written to Hercule Poirot.

'My friend Hastings will tell you that from the moment I received the first letter I was upset and disturbed. It seemed to me at once that there was something very wrong about the letter.'

'You were quite right,' said Franklin Clarke dryly.

'Yes. But there, at the very start, I made a grave error. I permitted my feeling – my very strong feeling about the letter – to remain a mere impression. I treated it as though it had been an intuition. In a well-balanced, reasoning mind there is no such thing as an intuition – an inspired guess! You *can* guess, of course – and a guess is either right or wrong. If it is right you call it an intuition. If it is wrong you usually do not speak of it again. But what is often called an intuition is really *an impression based on logical deduction or experience.* When an expert feels that there is something wrong about a picture or a piece of furniture or the signature on a cheque he is really basing that feeling on a host of small signs and details. He has no need to go into them minutely – his experience obviates that – the net result is *the definite impression that something is wrong*. But it is not a *guess*, it is an impression based on *experience*.

'*Eh bien*, I admit that I did not regard that first letter in the way I should. It just made me extremely uneasy. The police regarded it as a hoax. I myself took it seriously. I was convinced that a murder would take place in Andover as stated. As you know, a murder *did* take place.

'There was no means at that point, as I well realized, of knowing who the *person* was who had done the deed. The only course open to me was to try and understand just what kind of a person had done it.

'I had certain indications. The letter – the manner of the crime – the person murdered. What I had to discover was: the motive of the crime, the motive of the letter.'

'Publicity,' suggested Clarke.

'Surely an inferiority complex covers that,' added Thora Grey.

'That was, of course, the obvious line to take. But why *me? Why Hercule Poirot?* Greater publicity could be ensured by sending the letters to Scotland Yard. More again by sending them to a newspaper. A newspaper might not print the first letter, but by the time the second crime took place, A B C could have been assured of all the publicity the press could give. Why, then, Hercule Poirot? Was it for some *personal* reason? There was, discernible in the letter, a slight anti-foreign bias – but not enough to explain the matter to my satisfaction.

'Then the second letter arrived – and was followed by the murder of Betty Barnard at Bexhill. It became clear now (what I had already suspected) that the murders were to proceed on an alphabetical plan, but the fact, which seemed final to most people, left the main question unaltered to my mind. Why did A B C *need* to commit these murders?'

Megan Barnard stirred in her chair.

'Isn't there such a thing as – as a blood lust?' she said.

Poirot turned to her.

'You are quite right, mademoiselle. There *is* such a thing. The lust to kill. But that did not quite fit the facts of the case. A homicidal maniac who desires to kill usually desires to kill *as many victims as possible.* It is a recurring *craving*. The great idea of such a killer is to *hide his tracks* – not to *advertise* them. When we consider the four victims selected – or at any rate three of them (for I know very little of Mr Downes or Mr Earlsfield), we realize that *if he had chosen,* the murderer could have done away with them without incurring any suspicion. Franz Ascher, Donald Fraser or Megan Barnard, possibly Mr Clarke – those are the people the police would have suspected even if they had been unable to get direct proof. An unknown homicidal murderer would not have been thought of! Why, then, did the murderer feel it necessary to call attention to himself? Was it the necessity of leaving on each body a copy of an A B C railway guide? Was *that* the compulsion? Was there some complex connected *with the railway guide*?

'I found it quite inconceivable at this point *to enter into the mind of the murderer*. Surely it could not be magnanimity? A horror of responsibility for the crime being fastened on an innocent person?

'Although I could not answer the main question, certain things I did feel I was learning about the murderer.'

'Such as?' asked Fraser.

'To begin with – that he had a tabular mind. His crimes were listed by alphabetical progression – that was obviously important to him. On the other hand, he had no particular taste in victims – Mrs Ascher, Betty Barnard, Sir Carmichael Clarke, they all differed widely from each other. There was no sex complex – no particular age complex, and that seemed to me to be a very curious fact. If a man kills indiscriminately it is usually because he removes anyone who stands in his way or annoys him. *But the alphabetical progression showed that such was not the case here*. The other type of killer usually selects *a particular type of victim* – nearly always of the opposite sex. There was something haphazard about the procedure of A B C that seemed to me to be at war with the alphabetical selection.

'One slight inference I permitted myself to make. The choice of the A B C suggested to me what I may call a *railway-minded man*. This is more common in men than women. Small boys love trains better than small girls do. It might be the sign, too, of an in some ways undeveloped mind. The "boy" motif still predominated.

'The death of Betty Barnard and the manner of it gave me certain other indications. The manner of her death was particularly suggestive. (Forgive me, Mr Fraser.) To begin with, she was strangled with her own belt – therefore she must almost certainly have been killed by someone with whom she was on friendly or affectionate terms. When I learnt something of her character a picture grew up in my mind.

'Betty Barnard was a flirt. She liked attention from a personable male. Therefore A B C, to persuade her to come out with him, must have had a certain amount of attraction – of *le sex appeal!* He must be able, as you English say, to "get off". He must be capable of the click! I visualize the scene on the beach thus: the man admires her belt. She takes it off, he passes it playfully round her neck – says, perhaps, "I shall strangle you." It is all very playful. She giggles – and he pulls –'

Donald Fraser sprang up. He was livid.

'M. Poirot – for God's sake.'

Poirot made a gesture.

'It is finished. I say no more. It is over. We pass to the next murder, that of Sir Carmichael Clarke. Here the murderer goes back to his first method – the blow on the head. The same alphabetical complex – but one fact worries me a little. To be consistent the murderer should have chosen his towns in some definite sequence.

'If Andover is the 155th name under A, then the B crime should be the 155th also – or it should be the 156th and the C the 157th. Here again the towns seemed to be chosen in rather too *haphazard* a fashion.'

'Isn't that because you're rather biased on that subject, Poirot?' I suggested. 'You yourself are normally methodical and orderly. It's almost a disease with you.'

'No, it is *not* a disease! *Quelle idée!* But I admit that I may be over-stressing that point. *Passons!*

'The Churston crime gave me very little extra help. We were unlucky over it, since the letter announcing it went astray, hence no preparations could be made.

'But by the time the D crime was announced, a very formidable system of defence had been evolved. It must have been obvious that A B C could not much longer hope to get away with his crimes.

'Moreover, it was at this point that the clue of the

stockings came into my hand. It was perfectly clear that the presence of an individual selling stockings on and near the scene of each crime could not be a coincidence. Hence the stocking-seller must be the murderer. I may say that his description, as given me by Miss Grey, did not quite correspond with my own picture of the man who strangled Betty Barnard.

'I will pass over the next stages quickly. A fourth murder was committed – the murder of a man named George Earlsfield – it was supposed in mistake for a man named Downes, who was something of the same build and who was sitting near him in the cinema.

'*And now at last comes the turn of the tide.* Events play against A B C instead of into his hands. He is marked down – hunted – and at last arrested.

'The case, as Hastings says, is ended!

'True enough as far as the public is concerned. The man is in prison and will eventually, no doubt, go to Broadmoor. There will be no more murders. Exit! Finis! R.I.P.

'*But not for me!* I know nothing – nothing at all! Neither the *why* nor the *wherefore*.

'And there is one small vexing fact. The man Cust has an alibi for the night of the Bexhill crime.'

'That's been worrying me all along,' said Franklin Clarke.

'Yes. It worried me. For the alibi, it has the air

of being *genuine*. But it cannot be genuine unless – and now we come to two very interesting speculations.

'Supposing, my friends, that while Cust committed *three* of the crimes – the A, C, and D crimes – *he did not commit the B crime*.'

'M. Poirot. It isn't –'

Poirot silenced Megan Barnard with a look.

'Be quiet, mademoiselle. I am for the truth, I am! I have done with lies. Supposing, I say, *that A B C did not commit the second crime*. It took place, remember, in the early hours of the 25th – the day he had arrived for the crime. Supposing someone had forestalled him? What in those circumstances would he do? Commit a *second* murder, or lie low and *accept the first as a kind of macabre present?*'

'M. Poirot!' said Megan. 'That's a fantastic thought! All the crimes *must* have been committed by the same person!'

He took no notice of her and went steadily on:

'Such a hypothesis had the merit of explaining one fact – *the discrepancy between the personality of Alexander Bonaparte Cust* (who could never have made the click with any girl) *and the personality of Betty Barnard's murderer*. And it has been known, before now, that would-be murderers *have* taken advantage of the crimes committed by other people. Not all the crimes of Jack the Ripper were committed by Jack the Ripper, for instance. So far, so good.

'But then I came up against a definite difficulty.

'Up to the time of the Barnard murder, *no facts about the A B C murders had been made public.* The Andover murder had created little interest. The incident of the open railway guide had not even been mentioned in the press. It therefore followed that whoever killed Betty Barnard *must have had access to facts known only to certain persons* – myself, the police, and certain relations and neighbours of Mrs Ascher.

'That line of research seemed to lead me up against a blank wall.'

The faces that looked at him were blank too. Blank and puzzled.

Donald Fraser said thoughtfully:

'The police, after all, are human beings. And they're good-looking men –'

He stopped, looking at Poirot inquiringly.

Poirot shook his head gently.

'No – it is simpler than that. I told you that there was a second speculation.

'Supposing that Cust was *not* responsible for the killing of Betty Barnard? Supposing that *someone else* killed her. Could that someone else have been responsible *for the other murders too*?'

'But that doesn't make sense!' cried Clarke.

'Doesn't it? I did then *what I ought to have done at first*. I examined the letters I had received from a totally different point of view. I had felt from the beginning that there was something wrong with them – just as a picture expert knows a picture is wrong . . .

'I had assumed, without pausing to consider, that what was wrong with them was the fact that they were written by a madman.

'Now I examined them again – and this time I came to a totally different conclusion. What was wrong with them was *the fact that they were written by a sane man*!'

'What?' I cried.

'But yes – just that precisely! They were wrong as a picture is wrong – *because they were a fake*! They pretended to be the letters of a madman – of a homicidal lunatic, but in reality they were nothing of the kind.'

'It doesn't make sense,' Franklin Clarke repeated.

'*Mais si!* One must reason – reflect. What would be the object of writing such letters? To focus attention on the writer, to call attention to the murders! *En vérité*, it did not seem to make sense at first sight. And then I saw light. It was to focus attention on several murders – on a *group* of murders . . . Is it not your great Shakespeare who has said "You cannot see the trees for the wood."'

I did not correct Poirot's literary reminiscences. I

was trying to see his point. A glimmer came to me. He went on:

'When do you notice a pin least? When it is in a pin-cushion! When do you notice an individual murder least? When it is one of *a series of related murders*.

'I had to deal with an intensely clever, resourceful murderer – reckless, daring and a thorough gambler. *Not* Mr Cust! He could never have committed these murders! No, I had to deal with a very different stamp of man – a man with a boyish temperament (witness the schoolboy-like letters and the railway guide), an attractive man to women, and a man with a ruthless disregard for human life, a man who was necessarily a prominent person in *one* of the crimes!

'Consider when a man or woman is killed, what are the questions that the police ask? Opportunity. Where everybody was at the time of the crime? Motive. Who benefited by the deceased's death? If the motive and the opportunity are fairly obvious, what is a would-be murderer to do? Fake an alibi – that is, manipulate *time* in some way? But that is always a hazardous proceeding. Our murderer thought of a more fantastic defence. Create a *homicidal* murderer!

'I had now only to review the various crimes and find the possible guilty person. The Andover crime? The most likely suspect for that was Franz Ascher, but I could not imagine Ascher inventing and carrying out such an elaborate scheme, nor could I see him planning a premeditated murder. The Bexhill crime? Donald Fraser was a possibility. He had brains and ability, and a methodical turn of mind. But his motive for killing his sweetheart could only be jealousy – and jealousy does not tend to premeditation. Also I learned that he had his holidays *early* in August, which rendered it unlikely he had anything to do with the Churston crime. We come to the Churston crime next – and at once we are on infinitely more promising ground.

'Sir Carmichael Clarke was an immensely wealthy man. Who inherits his money? His wife, who is dying, has a life interest in it, and it then goes to *his brother Franklin*.'

Poirot turned slowly round till his eyes met those of Franklin Clarke.

'I was quite sure then. The man I had known a long time in my secret mind *was the same as the man whom I had known as a person. A B C and Franklin Clarke were one and the same!* The daring adventurous character, the roving life, the partiality for England that had showed itself, very faintly, in the jeer at foreigners. The attractive free and easy manner – nothing easier for him than to pick up a girl in a café. The methodical tabular mind – he made a list here one day, ticked off over the headings A B C – and finally, the boyish mind – mentioned by Lady Clarke and even shown by his taste in fiction – I have ascertained that there is a book in the library called *The Railway Children* by E. Nesbit. I had no further doubt in my own mind – A B C, the man who wrote the letters and committed the crimes, was *Franklin Clarke*.'

Clarke suddenly burst out laughing.

'Very ingenious! And what about our friend Cust, caught red-handed? What about the blood on his coat? And the knife he hid in his lodgings? He may deny he committed the crimes –'

Poirot interrupted.

'You are quite wrong. He admits the fact.'

'What?' Clarke looked really startled.

'Oh, yes,' said Poirot gently. 'I had no sooner spoken to him than I was aware that Cust *believed himself to be guilty*.'

'And even that didn't satisfy M. Poirot?' said Clarke.

'No. Because as soon as I saw him *I also knew that he could not be guilty*! He has neither the nerve nor the daring – nor, I may add, the *brains* to plan! All along I have been aware of the dual personality of the murderer. Now I see wherein it consisted. Two people were involved – the real murderer, cunning, resourceful and daring – and the *pseudo* murderer, stupid, vacillating and suggestible.

'Suggestible – it is in that word that the mystery of Mr Cust consists! It was not enough for you, Mr Clarke, to devise this plan of a *series* to distract attention from a *single* crime. You had also to have a stalking horse.

'I think the idea first originated in your mind as the result of a chance encounter in a city coffee den with this odd personality with his bombastic Christian names. You were at that time turning over in your mind various plans for the murder of your brother.'

'Really? And why?'

'Because you were seriously alarmed for the future. I do not know whether you realize it, Mr Clarke, but you played into my hands when you showed me a certain letter written to you by your brother. In it he displayed very clearly his affection and absorption in Miss Thora Grey. His regard may have been a paternal one – or he may have preferred to think it so. Nevertheless, there was a very real danger that on the death of your sister-in-law he might, in his loneliness, turn to this beautiful girl for sympathy and comfort and it might end – as so often happens with elderly men – in his marrying her. Your fear was increased by your knowledge of Miss Grey. You are, I fancy, an excellent, if somewhat cynical judge of character. You judged, whether correctly or not, that Miss Grey was a type of young woman "on the make". You had no doubt that she would jump at the chance of becoming Lady Clarke. Your brother was an extremely healthy and vigorous man. There might be children and your chance of inheriting your brother's wealth would vanish.

'You have been, I fancy, in essence a disappointed man all your life. You have been the rolling stone – and you have gathered very little moss. You were bitterly jealous of your brother's wealth.

'I repeat then that, turning over various schemes in your mind, your meeting with Mr Cust gave you an idea. His bombastic Christian names, his account of his epileptic seizures and of his headaches, his whole shrinking and insignificant personality, struck you as fitting him for the tool you wanted. The whole alphabetical plan sprang into your mind – Cust's initials – the fact that your brother's name began with a C and that he lived at Churston were the nucleus of the scheme. You even went so far as to hint to Cust at his possible end – though you could hardly hope that that suggestion would bear the rich fruit that it did!

'Your arrangements were excellent. In Cust's name you wrote for a large consignment of hosiery to be sent to him. You yourself sent a number of A B C's looking like a similar parcel. You wrote to him – a typed letter purporting to be from the same firm offering him a good salary and commission. Your plans were so well laid beforehand that you typed all the letters that were sent subsequently, *and then presented him with the machine on which they had been typed.*

'You had now to look about for two victims whose names began with A and B respectively and who lived at places also beginning with those same letters.

'You hit on Andover as quite a likely spot and your preliminary reconnaissance there led you to select Mrs Ascher's shop as the scene of the first crime. Her name was written clearly over the door, and you found by experiment that she was usually alone in the shop. Her murder needed nerve, daring and reasonable luck.

'For the letter B you had to vary your tactics. Lonely women in shops might conceivably have been warned. I should imagine that you frequented a few cafés and tea-shops, laughing and joking with the girls there and finding out whose name began with the right letter and who would be suitable for your purpose.

'In Betty Barnard you found just the type of girl you were looking for. You took her out once or twice, explaining to her that you were a married man, and that outings must therefore take place in a somewhat hole-and-corner manner.

'Then, your preliminary plans completed, you set to work! You sent the Andover list to Cust, directing him to go there on a certain date, and you sent off the first A B C letter to me.

'On the appointed day you went to Andover – and killed Mrs Ascher – without anything occurring to damage your plans.

'Murder No. 1 was successfully accomplished.

'For the second murder, you took the precaution of committing it, in reality, *the day before*. I am fairly certain that Betty Barnard was killed well before midnight on the 24th July.

'We now come to murder No. 3 – the important – in fact, the *real* murder from your point of view.

'And here a full meed of praise is due to Hastings, who made a simple and obvious remark to which no attention was paid.

'He suggested that the third letter went astray intentionally!

'And he was right! . . .

'In that one simple fact lies the answer to the question that has puzzled me so all along. Why were the letters addressed in the first place to Hercule Poirot, a private detective, and not to the police?

'Erroneously I imagined some personal reason.

'Not at all! The letters were sent to me because the essence of your plan was that one of them *should be wrongly addressed and go astray* – but you cannot arrange for a letter addressed to the Criminal Investigation Department of Scotland Yard to go astray! It is necessary to have a *private* address. You chose me as a fairly well-known person, and a person who was sure to take the letters to the police – and also, in your rather insular mind, you enjoyed scoring off a foreigner.

'You addressed your envelope very cleverly – Whitehaven – Whitehorse – quite a natural slip. Only Hastings was sufficiently perspicacious to disregard subtleties and go straight for the obvious!

'Of course the letter was *meant* to go astray! The police were to be set on the trail *only when the murder was safely over.* Your brother's nightly walk provided you with the opportunity. And so successfully had the A B C terror taken hold on the public mind that the possibility of your guilt never occurred to anyone.

'After the death of your brother, of course, your object was accomplished. You had no wish to commit any more murders. On the other hand, if the murders stopped without reason, a suspicion of the truth might come to someone.

'Your stalking horse, Mr Cust, had so successfully lived up to his role of the invisible – because insignificant – man, that so far no one had noticed that the same person had been seen in the vicinity of the three murders! To your annoyance, even his visit to Combeside had not been mentioned. The matter had passed completely out of Miss Grey's head.

'Always daring, you decided that one more murder must take place but this time the trail must be well blazed.

'You selected Doncaster for the scene of operations.

'Your plan was very simple. You yourself would

be on the scene in the nature of things. Mr Cust would be ordered to Doncaster by his firm. Your plan was to follow him round and trust to opportunity. Everything fell out well. Mr Cust went to a cinema. That was simplicity itself. You sat a few seats away from him. When he got up to go, you did the same. You pretended to stumble, leaned over and stabbed a dozing man in the row in front, slid the A B C on to his knees and managed to collide heavily with Mr Cust in the darkened doorway, wiping the knife on his sleeve and slipping it into his pocket.

'You were not in the least at pains to choose a victim whose name began with D. Anyone would do! You assumed – and quite rightly – that it would be considered to be a *mistake*. There was sure to be someone whose name began with D not far off in the audience. It would be assumed that he had been intended to be the victim.

'And now, my friends, let us consider the matter from the point of view of the false A B C – from the point of view of Mr Cust.

'The Andover crime means nothing to him. He is shocked and surprised by the Bexhill crime – why, he himself was there about the time! Then comes the Churston crime and the headlines in the newspapers. An A B C crime at Andover when he was there, an A B C crime at Bexhill, and now another close by . . .

Three crimes *and he has been at the scene of each of them.* Persons suffering from epilepsy often have blanks when they cannot remember what they have done . . . Remember that Cust was a nervous, highly neurotic subject and extremely suggestible.

'Then he receives the order to go to Doncaster.

'Doncaster! And the next A B C crime is to be in Doncaster. He must have felt as though it was fate. He loses his nerve, fancies his landlady is looking at him suspiciously, and tells her he is going to Cheltenham.

'He goes to Doncaster because it is his duty. In the afternoon he goes to a cinema. Possibly he dozes off for a minute or two.

'Imagine his feelings when on his return to his inn he discovers *that there is blood on his coat sleeve and a blood-stained knife in his pocket.* All his vague forebodings leap into certainty.

'*He – he himself – is the killer!* He remembers his headaches – his lapses of memory. He is quite sure of the truth – *he, Alexander Bonaparte Cust, is a homicidal lunatic.*

'His conduct after that is the conduct of a hunted animal. He gets back to his lodgings in London. He is safe there – known. They think he has been in Cheltenham. He has the knife with him still – a thoroughly stupid thing to do, of course. He hides it behind the hall stand.

'Then, one day, he is warned that the police are coming. It is the end! They *know*!

'The hunted animal does his last run . . .

'I don't know why he went to Andover – a morbid desire, I think, to go and look at the place where the crime was committed – the crime *he* committed though he can remember nothing about it . . .

'He has no money left – he is worn out . . . his feet lead him of his own accord to the police station.

'But even a cornered beast will fight. Mr Cust fully believes that he did the murders but he sticks strongly to his plea of innocence. And he holds with desperation to that alibi for the second murder. At least that cannot be laid to his door.

'As I say, when I saw him, I knew at once that he was *not* the murderer and that my name *meant* nothing to *him*. I knew, too, that he *thought* himself the murderer!

'After he had confessed his guilt to me, I knew more strongly than ever that my own theory was right.'

'Your theory,' said Franklin Clarke, 'is absurd!'

Poirot shook his head.

'No, Mr Clarke. You were safe enough *so long as no one suspected you*. Once you *were* suspected proofs were easy to obtain.'

'Proofs?'

'Yes. I found the stick that you used in the Andover

and Churston murders in a cupboard at Combeside. An ordinary stick with a thick knob handle. A section of wood had been removed and melted lead poured in. Your photograph was picked out from half a dozen others by two people who saw you leaving the cinema when you were supposed to be on the race-course at Doncaster. You were identified at Bexhill the other day by Milly Higley and a girl from the Scarlet Runner Roadhouse, where you took Betty Barnard to dine on the fatal evening. And finally – most damning of all – you *overlooked a most elementary precaution.* You left a fingerprint on Cust's typewriter – the typewriter that, if you are innocent, you *could never have handled.*'

Clarke sat quite still for a minute, then he said:

'*Rouge, impair, manque!* – you win, M. Poirot! But it was worth trying!'

With an incredibly rapid motion he whipped out a small automatic from his pocket and held it to his head.

I gave a cry and involuntarily flinched as I waited for the report.

But no report came – the hammer clicked harmlessly.

Clarke stared at it in astonishment and uttered an oath.

'No, Mr Clarke,' said Poirot. 'You may have noticed I had a new manservant today – a friend of mine – an expert sneak thief. He removed your pistol from your pocket, unloaded it, and returned it, all without you being aware of the fact.'

'You unutterable little jackanapes of a foreigner!' cried Clarke, purple with rage.

'Yes, yes, that is how you feel. No, Mr Clarke, no easy death for you. You told Mr Cust that you had had near escapes from drowning. You know what that means – that you were born for another fate.'

'You –'

Words failed him. His face was livid. His fists clenched menacingly.

Two detectives from Scotland Yard emerged from the next room. One of them was Crome. He advanced and uttered his time-honoured formula: 'I warn you that anything you say may be used as evidence.'

'He has said quite enough,' said Poirot, and he added to Clarke: 'You are very full of an insular superiority, but for myself I consider your crime not an English crime at all – not above-board – not *sporting* –'

Chapter 35

Finale

I am sorry to relate that as the door closed behind Franklin Clarke I laughed hysterically.

Poirot looked at me in mild surprise.

'It's because you told him his crime was not sporting,' I gasped.

'It was quite true. It was abominable – not so much the murder of his brother – but the cruelty that condemned an unfortunate man to a living death. *To catch a fox and put him in a box and never let him go!* That is not *le sport*!'

Megan Barnard gave a deep sigh.

'I can't believe it – I can't. Is it true?'

'Yes, mademoiselle. The nightmare is over.'

She looked at him and her colour deepened.

Poirot turned to Fraser.

'Mademoiselle Megan, all along, was haunted by a fear that it was you who had committed the second crime.'

Donald Fraser said quietly:

'I fancied so myself at one time.'

'Because of your dream?' He drew a little nearer to the young man and dropped his voice confidentially. 'Your dream has a very natural explanation. It is that you find that already the image of one sister fades in your memory and that its place is taken by the other sister. Mademoiselle Megan replaces her sister in your heart, but since you cannot bear to think of yourself being unfaithful so soon to the dead, you strive to stifle the thought, to kill it! That is the explanation of the dream.'

Fraser's eyes went towards Megan.

'Do not be afraid to forget,' said Poirot gently. 'She was not so well worth remembering. In Mademoiselle Megan you have one in a hundred – *un coeur magnifique!*'

Donald Fraser's eyes lit up.

'I believe you are right.'

We all crowded round Poirot asking questions, elucidating this point and that.

'Those questions, Poirot? That you asked of everybody. Was there any point in them?'

'Some of them were *simplement une blague*. But I learnt one thing that I wanted to know – *that Franklin Clarke was in London when the first letter was posted* – and also I wanted to see his face when I asked my question of Mademoiselle Thora. He was off his guard. I saw all the malice and anger in his eyes.'

'You hardly spared my feelings,' said Thora Grey.

'I do not fancy you returned me a truthful answer, mademoiselle,' said Poirot dryly. 'And now your second expectation is disappointed. Franklin Clarke will not inherit his brother's money.'

She flung up her head.

'Is there any need for me to stay here and be insulted?'

'None whatever,' said Poirot and held the door open politely for her.

'That fingerprint clinched things, Poirot,' I said thoughtfully. 'He went all to pieces when you mentioned that.'

'Yes, they are useful – fingerprints.'

He added thoughtfully:

'I put that in to please you, my friend.'

'But, Poirot,' I cried, 'wasn't it *true*?'

'Not in the least, *mon ami*,' said Hercule Poirot.

II

I must mention a visit we had from Mr Alexander Bonaparte Cust a few days later. After wringing Poirot's hand and endeavouring very incoherently and unsuccessfully to thank him, Mr Cust drew himself up and said:

'Do you know, a newspaper has actually offered me a hundred pounds – *a hundred pounds* – for a brief account of my life and history – I – I really don't know what to do about it.'

'I should not accept a hundred,' said Poirot. 'Be firm. Say five hundred is your price. And do not confine yourself to one newspaper.'

'Do you really think – that I might –'

'You must realize,' said Poirot, smiling, 'that you are a very famous man. Practically the most famous man in England today.'

Mr Cust drew himself up still further. A beam of delight irradiated his face.

'Do you know, I believe you're right! Famous! In all the papers. I shall take your advice, M. Poirot. The money will be most agreeable – most agreeable. I shall have a little holiday . . . And then I want to give a nice wedding present to Lily Marbury – a dear girl – really a dear girl, M. Poirot.'

Poirot patted him encouragingly on the shoulder.

'You are quite right. Enjoy yourself. And – just a little word – what about a visit to an oculist? Those headaches, it is probably that you want new glasses.'

'You think that it may have been that all the time?'

'I do.'

Mr Cust shook him warmly by the hand.

'You're a very great man, M. Poirot.'

Poirot, as usual, did not disdain the compliment. He did not even succeed in looking modest.

When Mr Cust had strutted importantly out, my old friend smiled across at me.

'So, Hastings – we went hunting once more, did we not? *Vive le sport.*'

The Mysterious Affair At Styles

POIROT'S FIRST CASE

Agatha Christie

Peril to the detective who says: "It is so small – it does not matter…" Everything matters.'

When Emily Inglethorpe is found murdered, Captain Hastings calls for help from an old friend: a certain Belgian detective who has grown bored of retirement.

A shattered coffee cup, a splash of candle grease, a bed of begonias – only Poirot could unravel an ingenious crime from these few intriguing clues.

'Almost too ingenious.' *Times Literary Supplement*

ISBN-13 978-0-00-711927-1

Murder on the Orient Express

POIROT

Agatha Christie

'The murderer is with us – on the train now…'

Just after midnight, the famous *Orient Express* is stopped in its tracks by a snowdrift. By morning, Hercule Poirot knows that the millionaire Simon Ratchett lies dead in his compartment, stabbed a dozen times, his door locked from the inside. One of his fellow passengers must be the murderer.

Isolated by the storm and with a killer in their midst, detective Hercule Poirot must find the killer amongst a dozen of the dead man's enemies, before the murderer decides to strike again…

'Very real, and keeps readers enthralled and guessing to the end.' *Times Literary Supplement*

ISBN-13 978-0-00-711931-8

Five Little Pigs

POIROT

Agatha Christie

Beautiful Caroline Crale was convicted of poisoning her husband, but just like the nursery rhyme, there were five other 'little pigs' who could have done it: Philip Blake (the stockbroker) who went to market; Meredith Blake (the amateur herbalist) who stayed at home; Elsa Greer (the three-time divorcee) who had her roast beef; Cecilia Williams (the devoted governess) who had none; and Angela Warren (the disfigured sister) who cried all the way home.

Sixteen years later, Caroline's daughter is determined to prove her mother's innocence, and Poirot just can't get that nursery rhyme out of his mind…

'Mrs Christie as usual puts a ring through the reader's nose and leads him to one of her smashing last-minute showdowns.' *Observer*

'The answer to the riddle is brilliant.'
Times Literary Supplement

ISBN-13 978-0-00-712073-4

Lord Edgware Dies

POIROT

Agatha Christie

When Lord Edgware is found murdered the police are baffled. His estranged actress wife was seen to visit him just before his death and Poirot himself heard her brag of her plan to 'get rid' of him.

After all, how could Jane have stabbed Lord Edgware to death in his library at exactly the same time she was seen dining with friends? It's a case that almost proves to be too much for the great Hercule Poirot.

'The whole case is a triumph of Poirot's special qualities.'
Times Literary Supplement

ISBN-13 978-0-00-712074-1

Evil Under the Sun

POIROT

Agatha Christie

The beautiful bronzed body of Arlena Stuart lay face down on the beach. But strangely, there was no sun and Arlena was not sun-bathing... she had been strangled.

Ever since Arlena's arrival the air had been thick with sexual tension. Each of the guests had a motive to kill her, including Arlena's new husband, but Hercule Poirot suspects that this apparent 'crime of passion' conceals something more evil and pre-meditated altogether.

'She springs her secret like a land mine.'

Times Literary Supplement

ISBN-13 978-0-00-711926-4